Behind
These
Hands

a novel in verse

LINDA VIGEN PHILLIPS

Light

Durh

Behind These Hands
Linda Vigen Phillips
lightmessages.com/linda-phillips

Published 2018, by Light Messages

www.lightmessages.com
Durham, NC 27713 USA
SAN: 920-9298

Paperback ISBN: 978-1-61153-259-3
E-book ISBN: 978-1-61153-258-6
Library of Congress Control Number: 2018933744

To Anna and Luke,

who already know how to celebrate life
with their hands.

Autumn

THE TOCCATA IN D MINOR

Late afternoon sun
slants through the windows
in dancing patterns.
Trees full of tired leaves
sway outside in a humid
September wind,

the kind of wind that
brings hurricanes to these parts.

Bach's Toccata in D Minor
lifts off the keyboard,
not by itself
like an old-fashioned player piano,

but because practiced fingers,

fingers that Dad said were born
            fourteen years ago
for precisely this purpose,

know the exact moment to strike,
the exact moment to lift.

Playing this piece creates
its own hurricane in my head.
Maybe dark for a moment
and eerie
then rising above the storm.
A storm that ends
not with destruction
but depletion,
exhaustion,
relief.

I finish the piece and stare
down at these long, slender fingers
that seem to have already made important
life decisions
without much input from me.

I'm about ready to start a conversation—
me with my hands and fingers—
when I hear a sound
growing painfully familiar:

Davy bumping into the doorway

on his way from the kitchen,
letting out with a loud "ouch"
before plopping into the chair
next to the piano.

"Can you teach me *now*, Claire?
Please, can you?"

I watch an orange popsicle
drip down his wrist.
I jump up to catch it with
a ragged Kleenex from my pocket.

"Your hands are sticky and
I have homework, Bud.
Another time, okay?"

"That's what you always say."

He sidles off the chair and stumbles up
the stairs, leaving an orange trail
on the hardwood floor.

"I don't always say you have sticky

fingers," I mutter under my breath.

But it's true.
I always say something to put him off
because otherwise I would have to face
trying to teach my nearly blind,
learning-disabled brother
how to play the Toccata
and that thought
overwhelms
me.

THE BROTHERS

Davy wasn't always visually impaired.
That's what they call him at school
since his eyesight started going bad last year.

I was seven when he was born,
perfect in every way,
chubby,
smiling all the time.
I used to ask Mom why he didn't cry much.
She just told me to enjoy it
while it lasts.
It has lasted all these years
even when his eyesight started going bad

and now

       they say he has a learning disorder,

          but he just keeps smiling.

It bothers me
that he smiles so much,

maybe because it doesn't seem
normal;

maybe because I know for sure
if I were in his shoes
my smile
would be the first to go.

Trent smiles, too,
but it's more often like
the sun that comes out after a storm.
Fiercely competitive at the age of six,
especially in anything athletic,
it takes some work on everybody's part
to get him to smile
after he loses at anything.
But even at his young age
he rarely loses.
He's that competitive.

I hear them upstairs in Davy's room
playing Nintendo.
The bleeps and clicks,
wah wahs, kerpows,
scale runs announcing
down
      the
              flagpole
      or
power up,
form their own familiar music,
and for now
it is a peaceful,
harmonious duet.

Davy must be smiling along
with Trent's triumphs.

"THE KITE"

I move the something-interesting-casserole
from fridge to oven and set the time
and temperature.

It's faculty meeting day for Mom
and Wind Ensemble practice for Dad
which means one of them
did pre-dinner cooking before dawn.
They have teamwork and efficiency down
so well
it's hard to decide which one
contributed most
to my type-A,
power-driven,
ambitious
gene-pool.

I have time to get in some practice
before I make the salad
or before the melodic duo upstairs
deteriorates into
brotherly discord.
I ease onto the piano bench,
pause to breathe, straighten my posture
much as I do
before a recital, and let my fingers go
unleashed like puppies on an open beach.
I let them go wherever they want,
            and I talk to them.
(Only Juan knows I talk to my hands
and fingers. He and his flute fingers
are the only ones
who could *ever* relate.)

Let's fly.
     Sail.
          Soar.

                Don't let the wind catch up.

My composition, "The Kite,"
not yet put down on paper
but carving an increasingly firm
notch in my brain,
carries me back eight years to Nags Head
on a Carolina blue day
when it was just Mom and Dad
and me,
the flaming red and orange dragon kite,
and a roaring ocean wind
the week before first grade.

The taste of salt,
sand clinging to my bare feet,
my long hair trailing behind in the wind
like the dragon's tail,
the rising, dipping,
unpredictable flight path
and most of all
the lyrical, contagious laughter
of Mom
and Dad
and me.

I finish the piece, smiling.
Yes, I have it.
Yes, I am ready to write it down.
Yes, I am ready to record it.
Yes, I am ready to go after
        the most prestigious music contest
        in North Carolina.

JUAN

I picture Juan's composition
bursting out his open bedroom window
on these Autumn afternoons
like a soaring songbird.
When Juan practices, he loses himself
in his music
        totally,
just like I do.
Every breath he breathes
into his sterling silver Haynes
results in
        mysterious,
            magical
                music.

I haven't heard his piece
but I know it will be
genius material.

We've been best friends
and musical competitors
since our mothers signed us up
for piano lessons
at Mrs. Cobb's Music Studio
when we were five.
In the fourth grade Juan
discovered the flute,
but he says
piano will always be his first love.

He's taken first place
at just about every flute competition
he's ever entered.
When his parents got him
the sterling silver Haynes

two years ago,
he gave me his old Armstrong
and enough lessons
to play mess-around flute
with him when the mood strikes.

Now there's a new twist
and no time for jamming.
For the first time
        ever
we will compete against each other
in the NC Music Teachers' Association
composition competition.

Juan on the flute,
me on the piano,
there can be
        only
        one
        winner.

The thought of this
not being a good idea
gives me more butterflies
than the thought of
performing my own composition.

But Juan,
ever the punster,
        says we can both "Handel" it
and ever the competitor,
        says we should each pour all our energy
        into perfecting our own piece.

When I consulted my fingers
they agreed,

but my heart

isn't quite so sure.

MIA

I don't really consult Mia
about competing against Juan
because I already know
what she will say.

"Go for it, girl!"

Her confidence in me
exceeds
my confidence in me
most of the time.

My confidence in her
exceeds
my confidence in me
most of the time,
too.

What we have in common
is an unadulterated obsession
over the things we love most.
She's been writing stories,
      poems,
      plays,
      articles,
      and her mother's grocery list
since she was barely out of diapers,
or so she tells me.

You don't get to be yearbook editor,

and school newspaper editor,
and writing contest winner
        unless there's some truth to it.

She tries to get me to branch out,
        you know, write an article or two
        for the paper,

and I try to get her to appreciate the beauty
        of Bach's chorales,

but mostly we stay buried in our own worlds
and maintain our membership
in the mutual admiration society.

HOME AFTER SCHOOL

Mom arrives first
with the beaten down,
post-faculty-meeting look
that says "No problems please,
I've had enough for one day."

Trent comes barreling down the stairs
to reach for a hug
and announces that Donkey Kong
just had a major victory.
Davy follows, slower,
groping for the stair rail,
smiling.
"Hi, Mom."

She gives them both hugs.

I remember that the salad isn't made
and dart into the kitchen

before it becomes an issue.

Dad slams the door.
Mom, distracted by the boys,
forgets to call him on it.

"My cooking smells pretty good,
don't you think," he says with a wink
to the general population.

I smile,
the only one of the general population
who has heard his voice
in the mayhem
and observed his self-satisfied wink.

Mom comes into the kitchen,
a boy on each hip,
both vying for her attention.
She does a bang-up job
giving it to both
simultaneously.

After grace, Dad leans over
to help Davy find his fork
and get him oriented to the food
on his plate.

Trent jabbers away
about the tag football sign-ups,
and then Mom asks Davy
how his day went.
He smiles through a review
of the day at Gateway School
where the biggest news
revolves around Nick's
getting detention for wandering

off the playground to retrieve
a ball during recess.

"How did your spelling test go?"

Davy tries to spear some casserole
with his fork
and misses.

"Miss Daniels said she bets I'll get more
right next time."

"I know you will," Dad says,
exchanging a worried glance with Mom.
Davy pushes noodles onto his fork with his fingers.

Dinner is soon over.
Mom supervises homework;
Dad's in charge of baths.

I'm the cleanup crew,
        and since no one has asked,
                I talk to my hands about our composition
                        and the upcoming competition.

THE SCORE

The heavy practice-room door
shudders behind me.
I set a pile of blank sheet music
and my favorite #2 pencil
on the small table next to the piano.
I set my cell on vibrate,
breathe in,
breathe out,
straighten tall.

I close my eyes.
I can see
the late summer sun
blazing in that clear azure sky
and feel my toes dig into the sand.

"The Kite" takes off
in the dead silent stillness
of this tiny room
as if the breeze were driving
through these walls,
and I chase it with the melody
that has gelled in my brain
these weeks of practice,
experimentation,
frustration,
doubts,

and now

certainty
and
exhilaration.

I slide on the bench
to the little table,
and begin the task
of setting down the notes
that are strung across my brain,
ready to pluck down
like washing on a clothesline.

Tap-tap-tap.

Startled.
I stop to listen,
not sure at first

if the sound is real
        or in my head,
and just as I look toward the door
I see Tara lean in,
flashing her slightly overheated smile
as her long, golden hair falls
toward her perfectly made-up face.
She keeps one hand on the knob
and reaches around her head with the other
to hold her hair back.

"Oh, Claire, I'm so sorry to interrupt."

Then why did you?

"I thought when I couldn't find him,
he'd be here, but I see that he's not."

"You thought he would be here
in the same practice room with me
because...?"

"No, I mean I thought,
        you know,
he'd be around here practicing
like you are,
you know,
polishing his composition
like crazy
and I see that's *exactly* what *you're* doing
so I'll let you go.
Ohmygosh.
I see I've already been gone too long
from cheerleading practice anyway.
We all think it's so cute
how you two geniuses are going
after this big prize

against each other,
you know,
after all these years
of being so,
um,
close musically,
you know.
Ta Tah!"

It takes a few minutes
for the air to clear
after she closes the door,
sort of like when a car
with emission problems passes
you on the road.
You want to open the windows
and let the nasty fumes escape.

Breathe in.
Breathe out.
Get back to work
and forget...

"Oh,"
she bursts back in,
causing my heart to lurch.
"If he shows up, tell him
the late carpool pick-up
will meet on the upper field
at 6:00."

Breathe in.
Breathe out.

THE LOCKER

My locker is in the music wing
even though my instrument,
      piano,
doesn't get packed around
like Juan's flute.
I see him throughout the day
and that drives Tara crazy.

Funniest thing of all...
      Juan is oblivious,
            true nerd,
      to her idol worship.
The pleasure is all mine
      evil,
      ugly
      me.

RULES OF THE GAME

"Are you ready to roll, Claire?" Juan asks,
changing out math book for history.

"You mean *the piece*?"

He stands up tall, runs his hand through
thick, curly hair, and smiles big.

What I love about Juan is
      he does not have
      an insincere bone
      in his lanky Cuban body.

He really cares,
      really wants to know

how it's going
with me,

and part of me still wishes
I was competing against
anyone but him,
who has been like a brother to me
all these years.

"Yeah, I'm ready to record.
Feelin' pretty good.
How about you?"

He says the same.
We decided early on
not to exchange details
like titles,
melodic themes,
rhythms,
genres.
We are bound
by the contest rules:
        no longer than five minutes,
        score must be handwritten
        along with a recorded version.

We agree to a private
popcorn and world-premier session
after we both
meet the deadline.

SOMETHING MORE

I've set aside a week from Friday to record.
That means I have over a week
to practice,

practice,
       practice.

I'll stay after school
when it wouldn't be cool for anyone
to be hanging out in the halls,
      especially Tara,
      and I'll use the practice room.

I slide through the piece at home
on cruise control.
No fine tuning.
My mind drifts,
my hands do the driving,

wondering if Juan has already submitted
but not really wanting to know,
      wondering what Tara sees in Juan
      when she has the pick of the jocks,
        wondering what she'd say
        if I called her on it one day,
          wondering...

Slam!

I stop abruptly at the sound of the front door
shutting hard when no one is expected home
this early
ever.

"Davy?"
I freeze on the piano bench
and hold my breath,
waiting for his voice.
His carpool usually drops him off first
but not
this early.

"Hi, Claire."

I turn around in time to see
Davy slip upstairs.
Tired-looking Mom
motions for me to follow her
to the kitchen.

"What is it, Mom?
Is something the matter?"

She pulls off her shoes,
sets the kettle on for tea,
hops up on a bar stool,
and sighs heavily.

"We've had a day, Davy and I.
I haven't wanted to worry you, Claire.
Several weeks ago the school called
with more concerns, *again.*
  Davy's been stumbling too much.
  Davy's falling further behind in everything,
    especially math.
  When was the last time you had his eyes checked?
So we did it all again today
with another specialist,
a pediatric neurologist.

My mom,
stronger than steel,
fights to hold back tears.

She doesn't have the answers
to any of my questions.
  What are they looking for?
  How much worse is he?

So we drink tea
in silence.

WAITING

You could slice it with a knife,
        the tension in our house.
No, not in our house,
        between Mom and Dad.

Sudden,
the tension seems so sudden,
but if I climb out of my musical delirium
long enough to look back,
it's been building for a while,
maybe months.

Mom
has always earned a D- for patience.
She'll be the first to agree
and on good days,
laughingly wonders how she ever ended up
teaching.

Funny
thing is, classroom tension bears no resemblance
to waiting for a call
from the doctor.

Dad,
on the other hand,
turns humor on so thick:
        jokes,
        puns,
        riddles,
        antics—

you almost wish for any kind of news
to break the phony fun.

They
aren't discussing
with me what kind of news
we are waiting for.

Words
wouldn't tell me
nearly as much
as the silent worry
I see in their eyes.

PAINFUL

Mia texts:

How's the winning piece coming?

I consider not answering
like I often do
when words don't seem
up to doing the job
of communicating
        pain,
        or embarrassment,
        or hurt,
        or anger,
        or anything emotionally big

nearly as well as music.

But my one good girlfriend, Mia
doesn't know how to speak that language

and all I can think to text is

Idk. Painful.

WAVERING IN THE WIND

"The Kite"
doesn't have enough wind
to keep it afloat today.

Dad finally asked how it was going
this morning at breakfast,
but I felt his thoughts fly off
before I could finish telling him
what I thought
        was the truth
              last week:
                    I'm on top of it.

Lately
I've been thinking how things evolved
        so fast
since that Labor Day weekend
when the contest leaped off the page
of Dad's music journal,
        the article about the winner
        of last year's NC Music Teachers' Association
        composition contest.
I stopped to read it
in the middle of packing
for a family outing,

fingers tingling
as if pulsing electrical charges
were sending a cryptic message
through the paper

directly to me.

This contest is for you!
I saw myself performing the winning piece,
      then spending the summer
       with the musical geniuses
at Duke, exploring digital production,
not to mention racking up the
$1,000 scholarship towards college.

The look on Dad's face
when I shared my exuberant decision
sent a different kind of tingling in my body,
      this one down my spine.

I couldn't get a reading
on what blipped so quickly
across the brain-space
of the head of the music department
at Coltrane Community College,
      usually my biggest fan.

Next thing I know Dad tells Juan
about the contest, something that hurt
at first.

Doesn't he want his own daughter
to have the best chance of winning?

Doesn't he know Juan and I
are too close
to be competing like this?

Doesn't he know
I'll probably lose?

But that's my dad.

Always wanting to give everyone
a fair shake.

I'm pounding out the Toccata
because I can't seem to concentrate
on "The Kite"

when Davy comes up behind me
and taps me on the back.

You wouldn't turn him down today,
would you, Claire?

"Hop up, Bud. Let's have that lesson."

His half smile takes on the intensity
of a sunrise, and I slide over on the bench.
I place Davy's fingers on the starting keys.
He starts humming the opening tune
that has been like a fixture in our house
during most of his lifetime.

I'm relieved my tears
fall into my lap,
        unnoticed
by the maestro.

RESOLVE

I wake up with a jolt,
beating the alarm by five minutes
to my 5:00 a.m. date with the day.

I *will* get to the practice lab
thanks to the coveted off-hours key
   Mr. Jenkins entrusts to a select few,

and Carlos's willingness to drive
    his brother and me to school
        on his way to pre-dawn athletic torture.

I *will* shake off the doom and gloom
    of worried-sick parents.

I *will* get my head straight.
I *will* get "The Kite" ready to fly
        before the deadline.

I will *not* let...what?
        Something   that probably has a simple answer,
                   that can be controlled by meds,
                   that might even be out-grow-able,
                   that surely can't be life threatening...

I *will* not let this ruin a chance of a lifetime.

Will I?

TRASHED IDEA

Clock runs a race.
Rampant thoughts
cloud my brain.

Fingers get the message
    due to conditions beyond our control
not before they push on to the end.

Rote,
    passionless,
        driving blind into the fog.

First bell sounds a warning.

I slam the keys hard
    finally mustering passion.

Discordant finale
to a trashed practice session.

Maybe a trashed idea?

AMBIVALENCE

It doesn't help,
the self-satisfied look
on Juan's face
at the lockers.

"Great practice session this morning, huh?"

Blank stare
diving for my books,
pushing down tears
he'll never understand.

"Oh, oh. Looks like you hit a snag?"

*He knows our family
like his own
and we've always been close,
so why don't I tell him?*

"We need to talk?"

*He'll think I'm bummed out
because of him—
our competing against each other,
so when I tell him the truth
he'll never believe me.*

"Lunch, the table near the door?"

I nod
and head for the cafeteria.

THE TRUTH

Juan slides onto the bench
two minutes after me.
Half a minute later
Tara's radar picks it up
from across the cafeteria
and reflects it back
with a sugar-coated, way-too-smiley wave
that only I catch.

Morning classes cleared my thoughts.
I need to air them out.

I'm just about ready to start talking
when Mia plops down.
I can't hide my disappointment,
and she starts to leave.

"Oops, I see I've interrupted something big."

I almost let her leave and then signal her to sit down.
What am I thinking? The three of us
have been like the musketeers
since third grade.

"It's Davy.
The house is on red alert
waiting for the doctor's report."

Juan interrupts. "What doctor's report?
                  What's going on?"

"The school has noticed significant changes recently.
 You know, a school for kids with learning disabilities
 is tuned into that stuff."

"Seems like he's had every test imaginable this past year."

"Exactly.
          Opthalmologists.
          Neurologists.
          Brain scans.
          Everything but a definite diagnosis.

My parents act like it can only be bad.
It ticks me off the way they are carrying on.
I mean, it could just be a glitch in his system
that meds can take care of, right?
It doesn't have to be the end of the world
or Davy's world,
does it?

I know he has a bum rap already,
losing vision at age seven,
learning difficulties.
          He doesn't need one more thing,
but until we know anything for sure
I just wish everyone could chill.
I can't concentrate.
I mean, the timing...
          That's it.
          It sucks."

Juan says, "Davy's situation or the contest?"

Davy, of course.

I chew extra long and hard
on my cardboard sandwich
and look away from my longtime friend's
see-through stare.

At least he didn't flat out ask me
if competing against him is the problem.

At least I didn't have to answer
to something I can't possibly sort out
right now.

"I'm so sorry, Claire," Mia says.
"I'm with you. Let's hope for a cool-down in your family
until you find out. In the meantime, poor Davy."

Her words sear.

*Where do I get off
feeling sorry for me?*

TEST RESULTS

The suspense is over.
Our house feels like
those pictures you see
after a tornado levels
           everything
but the victims are alive,
shuffling around the debris
in a daze.

It's called Batten disease.

Mom and Dad sat me down
between them

on the couch last night
      after Davy and Trent were in bed
and told me what they know
      or maybe
just what they want me to know.

The failing vision
and learning problems
      are part of it,

and

it's going to get worse:
      seizures,
      total blindness,
      physical and mental deterioration.
There is no cure.
He may not live to see twenty.
Before the end
everything,
      everything
            shuts
            down.

WHY

We all cry.
I've never seen my dad cry before,
but this is gut-wrenching sobbing,
      sobs that shake the couch cushions
      like a kid jumping on them
while mom weeps quietly and gropes
for a box of tissues.

I make them tell me again
      and again

what it all means
as if my brain can't absorb it all
in one terrible dose.

"Claire," Mom puts her arm around me
and finds my eyes. "The boys
are not to know any of this, do you
understand?"

I nod, unable to stop crying.

"It would serve no useful purpose," Dad says,
blowing his nose.

"But why?" I stammer.

"You mean why not tell them?" Mom says.

I try to pull myself together,
unable to define
what I mean
by
why.

Why Davy?
Why our family?
Why is this happening?
Why now?
Why do I have to carry this burden of silence?
Why can't the problem be fixed?

NEW NORMAL

I see immediately
how things have changed.
       Mom gives me something to help me sleep.

She tells me
we won't make this a habit.

"I know we put a lot on you tonight.
You have a deadline that is important
       to you
       and us,
and life needs to go on
       in this house,
       in this family,

and Dad and I love you so much."

She shakes two pills into her own hands
and we all turn our backs on
this horrible day.

THE NEXT DAY

The alarm triggers my thoughts
       abruptly
       like electricity coming on
       after an outage.

My brother is going to die
       young,
       sick,
       wasted
       before our eyes.

Last night didn't really happen,
       did it?

This can't be a school day.

My body feels like crap

four days to deadline,
        and I'm not ready to record.

How can I face Davy
        or Trent
and act normal
ever again?

BUSINESS AS USUAL

Dad's in the shower.
Mom's fixing the boys' lunches.
Davy's making a mess with his cereal,
        milk half in, half out of the bowl.
Trent slams his dish into the sink
        and races upstairs to get dressed
        without responding to Mom's
        "Hey, slow it down."

I'm gathering my book bag
when Carlos honks twice.

I give Mom a quick hug
without eye contact
and head for the door.

The only thing
out of the ordinary
on this new morning

is the inability to say Davy's name
without choking up.

They said I couldn't *say* anything
but they didn't say I couldn't
do something different.

I give my brother a silent hug
and dash out the door.

A GOOD DOSE OF TARA

First thing inside the car
my heart sinks.
I forgot it was Tuesday;
      Tara always rides with us
      on Tuesday.

Not only does my heart sink
but my stomach turns
at whatever she has slathered
somewhere on her body
to give off
such a sickening

fragrance.

And then there is the chatter
already in high gear
and not missing a beat
as I slide into the seat next to her.

It is, of course,
a cheerleading story.
Instead of listening
I stare, mesmerized by her
      long, thick, bottle-blond hair
          that sways like a heavy curtain
          powered by her body language;
      glossy lips totally color-coordinated with
      well-manicured nails;
      long, thick, black eyelashes

that flutter and accentuate
the orthodontic-perfect smile.
It's a total package of goodies
so foreign to me
(I forgot to mention the huge boobs)
that sitting next to her this morning
feels like being on the set
of a soap opera.

Mom sometimes says this about quirky things:
It was just what the doctor ordered.
Tara, good for my health.

A SECOND GOOD DOSE

Tara jumps out of the car first
and runs toward a cluster of pompom girls
with a hasty "See ya."
Juan and I head to the lockers.
He's laughing and scratching his head.

If there is a good joke, I want to hear it.

"Claire, want to hear something funny?
I think my big bro has the hots for Tara."

"Ya think?" I break into a
genuine fit of giggles.
"I take it you noticed
how he practically
rolled the car
while his eyes stayed glued
to the rear view mirror
during her cheerleading
monologue."

"Man, I about cracked up." Juan is laughing
deep belly laughs. "I was afraid if I looked
across the seat I'd decompose."

Juan laughs at his musical pun.
We both laugh and snicker
all the way to the lockers
and I realize
how good it feels

until I *remember*,
          and then I feel crazy
as I fight tears
so close behind
a good laugh.

A BAD FIT

On an ordinary day—
          the days before last night—

I could sail through classes
with music themes posing
the only significant distraction.

Today is different.
It feels like uncomfortable new shoes,
shoes someone else picked out for me,
shoes that pinch,
          rub,
          squeeze,
          burn.
Shoes that are ugly,
cost too much money,
and shoes I have to wear
someplace I don't want to go.

Shoes that hurt
make me think of Davy

and how he already has trouble
walking without bumping into something
because of his eyesight,
and now

I wonder how long he will
walk
       at
            all.

Today
there is no music
running through my head.

PRACTICE

Juan follows me to the practice rooms
and hollers for me to wait up.
We haven't talked since the morning laugh session,

but now

I really wish he would go to his cubicle
and leave me to my cubicle,
and we could both get on
with music contest preparation,

      life as it was

before yesterday.

I slam the door
      practically in his face

without a word,
while he stands
bewildered
at the window.

I slide onto the bench
and begin playing
something,
       anything
to let him know

I desperately need music right now.

Two minutes into
Rachmaninoff Concerto #2
I slam both hands down

hard,
discordant,
loud,

slip off the bench
onto the floor
crying,
       wailing uncontrollably,
beating my fists to the floor.
Why, why, why?

CONFESSION

Juan pushes the door open
in a rush
as if he might find
       blood and guts,
       broken appendages,
       or damaged piano parts.

He eases down on the floor
next to me and waits long minutes
        for the crying to end,
        for me to talk.

"It's the worst you can imagine,"
I say, and start crying again.

We both have a music deadline
and so much to do.
It's been a long day,
but Juan's earnest, kind eyes

tell me

he has all the time in the world
to listen.

"Davy," he says so firmly
it catches me off guard.
It's a statement, not a question.

I tell him all I know in a cascade
of jumbled words,
and end with something approaching confession:

how crappy I feel
for thinking Davy's death sentence
will mess up
my preparation
for the contest.

FEELING DIRTY

"Not *my man*," he says.
                It's what he's always called Davy
                since he was a toddler.

Juan cradles his head in his hands,
elbows digging into his crossed legs,
as if this position might help make sense
out of the words he just heard.

"Not *my man*."

I pull myself together.
Shock spreads across Juan's face
like a time-lapsed solar eclipse,
and tears pool in his dark eyes
as he struggles
with his own reaction.

He has the same questions I had
but mostly,
it's the big one that I can't answer:
                How long?
                How long does he have?

I shrug, take in a shaky breath,
rivet my eyes on the piano,
addressing the elephant in the room
with a burning glare.

Juan picks up on it.

"It's okay, Claire. Don't beat up on yourself.
Who wouldn't feel the same way right now?
I mean, jeez,
you've got this humongous deadline,

you've given it everything you have so far,
you're under a lot of pressure
and it's hard,
        hard as hell
        to concentrate."

I return his intense gaze
with a look of gratitude
and for a second,
        I believe he has a valid point,
but the truth sits like deadweight
at the bottom of my soul.

"Thanks, but it doesn't stop me from feeling
dirty inside."

AFTER-SCHOOL MAYHEM

I check my eyes for puffiness
as Carlos lets me out in the driveway,
then I feel a wave of nausea
when I realize puffy eyes
won't be noticed by Davy anyway.

It doesn't get past Mom's radar.
She gives me a concerned look
that gets lost in the after-school mayhem
of two screaming boys chasing each other
around the house over a Nintendo issue.

Dad from the family room: *Stop the noise I'm on the phone.*

Mom from the kitchen: *Claire, stir the soup while I deal with the boys.*

Me barely in the door: *Burn this moment into my brain:*

the shrieks,
the running,
the energy,
the life,
the urgency of silly boy-conflicts.

I want it to be like this

forever.

A FUNNY THING HAPPENED ON THE WAY TO...

Dad is at his most ridiculous best at dinner
and Mom lets it go on without the usual
reprimand to keep order at the table,
but I watch the concern about
eating and choking
in her vigilant gaze.

Dad: Anyone know how to make a bandstand?

We all chew and think.
My exhausted brain is betting one of my brothers
will get it before me.
Mom tells Dad this is too much of a play on words
and makes him explain what a bandstand is.
Dad hints that bandstand can also be two separate words,
band and stand,
        and he demonstrates the standing part.

Trent: Dad, if you didn't have a chair you would have
to eat standing up.

Dad: (Points and gestures "more" as in charades.)
        What would that do to the members of the band?

Trent: They would all be standing up to play.

Davy: A standing band, right Dad?

Dad: (His face flushed and almost glowing.)
        Exactly, Davy. You've almost got it. They would
        be standing because we took their...

Davy and Trent together: Chairs away!

Mom gets up to clear some plates,
        and from the kitchen
I hear muffled sniffles and nose blowing.

For the second time today
family, my family,
feels like a vocabulary word
that suddenly takes on
a whole new meaning.

DON'T QUESTION A GOOD THING

I wake from a good night's sleep
feeling rested,
        hopeful,
        confident,

ready to hammer out the rough edges
and launch—record—"The Kite"
        soon,
maybe even tomorrow if I can get in
a decent practice today.

I wonder
        as I comb the snarls out of my long, brown,
        non-Tara hair
why I feel so peaceful this morning.

Juan's pumped-up words of encouragement
　　　that I all but dissed,

and

the noise of Trent and Davy
in their boys-will-be-boys mode,

and

the dinner fun brought on
by Dad's ridiculous riddle...

It all added up to
things that filled my cup
at the end of a sad day,
and except for two minutes of Rachmaninoff,

the day was a musical void.

I decide to let that fact dangle as an observation
　　　to be pondered
　　　　　　on a more analytical day.

BLOOD WORK

The good feeling follows me downstairs
where once again
I welcome the morning chaos.
This time, Trent's protests about missing
flag football take center stage.
I don't tune in until
　　　I hear my name.

"Claire," Mom says
with a too-huge smile that doesn't match

the edge in her voice,
"I'm picking the boys up after school today
and we're all going to drop by
the doctor's office
to donate a few drops of our blood so that..."

> "and it won't be any worse than getting a shot,"
> Davy interrupts through a mouth full of cereal,
> parroting back what he's already heard this morning.

> "But I have to miss football and it's
> just not fair," shrieks Trent.

"...and as I was saying, doctors do this from time to time
so they can learn more about us
and treat us more effectively when,
        when we are sick
and yes, Davy, it's no worse than a shot,
and I'm sorry, Trent, but it's just one day
out of the season you'll miss
and Claire, I'll swing by right after I get them, at about
three..."

My heart lurches.
I feel dizzy, lightheaded.
        Maybe if I'm lucky
        I'll faint.
        She'll let me stay home.
        That's the only way
        I am ever going to get any practice in.

"...and I can swing back and drop you off at
the practice rooms if you want afterward, Claire,
because it won't take long and I know how much
you want to work on your piece."

Mom pauses to take in a deep breath.

I look at her
as the blood starts flowing back to my brain,
and I realize what really just hit me

wasn't about music
or getting much-needed practice,

it was about the realities
of Batten.

MUSIC MADNESS

In all the events of the past few days
it hadn't occurred to me to ask
    what about Trent and me?
Now the unanswered question
makes my stomach feel
like it's a wet wash cloth
being wrung out by someone's angry twists.

Mom drops me off
and tells me to text Dad when I'm ready
to be picked up. I head for the door
that my key opens.

I try warming up on one of my favorite *thinking* pieces,
    Handel's Sonata #7,
letting the quiet of the practice room calm me,
    thankful for a Mom who understands
    how I desperately needed this time.

I try to resist letting my thoughts
turn from wondering to worrying.

The bandage over the cotton wad

where they took my blood
pulls my thoughts to the samples our family
just dropped off at the lab.

> *...there is no cure;*
> *you may not live to see twenty;*
> *everything shuts down...*

I lunge off the bench,
thankful that no one is around
to see me pace in circles,
talking to myself like a crazy person,
      not just talking to my hands
      but to my whole being.
Talking myself,
      no, *SHOUTING* myself
out of Batten thoughts
and into music thoughts,

because

the only reality
in my life
that I am sure of
at this moment

is

to practice "The Kite"
into perfection.

TAKE "ONE"

By the fifth run-through
I'm feeling loose,
"The Kite" is soaring

49

finally,
and I'm setting up the recording equipment
when Mom texts:

Home soon? Getting late.

I'm shocked to see it's after 8:00 p.m.

Recording. Tell Dad side door at 9.

Can't stop now or I'll lose it.
        Sit tall.
        Flex fingers.
        Breathe deep.
        Hit 'record.'

I keep the image of "The Kite"
right before me
on the screen that I imagine
running across the top inside of my brain,
like one of those news tickers
with bright neon lights at Times Square.

The melody paints a picture
of warm afternoon sun,
strong wind coming in off the ocean,
whipping "The Kite" into a frenzy,
swirling and soaring,
spiraling to a near nose dive in the sand
before jetting skyward
and dancing above me
on a whimsical high current
with barely a tug on the string—

        and then

Davy's face appears across my inner screen

like a hologram,

and I totally lose it,
slam the off button,
sit on the bench holding my head
in my hands,
rocking back and forth
and saying every curse word
I've ever heard.

IT'S SIMPLY TOO HARD

I stand under the street light
so Dad won't have to remind me
        it's under the street light
        he expects me to stand
when he picks me up.

"Well?"

I turn towards him in the dark car,
trying to see what's behind the bite
in his voice.

Is it me,
his hectic job,
Davy,
all of the above?

"Well, what?"

Immediately I regret the sassy come back.
I face my palm towards him
like a traffic cop
before he does the same to me.

"Whoa, I'm sorry, Dad. I know what you
want to know, but I don't think you want to hear
all the fowl language I just let loose with
in the practice room when I let...
when I totally lost
all concentration
in the middle of recording.
It's no use. I can't do this."

I fight the tears.

Long silence.

"You know, honey,
it's okay with your mom and me
if you, if you..."

"Bail?" I can't decide if I want to hear this
from him
or not.
He tells me it's understandable
under these circumstances
to find it difficult
to concentrate
and maybe
I should give myself permission
to, yes,
          bail,
and wait for
things to quiet down.

Really?
Quiet down?
Blow over?
Get better
          when there is a time bomb ticking
          in our family now?

"You didn't want me to enter this contest in the first place,
did you, Dad?"

My question takes us both by surprise,
and so does his silence
that speaks volumes
and lasts all the way home.

I barely make it to my room
before letting the floodgates open.

It's
simply
too
hard.

SATURDAY AT THE PARK

It's Saturday.
      Long, deep breaths,
      easier said than done
      after yesterday's disastrous
      recording fiasco.

I start and delete text after text.
      First to Mia
      because she'll tell me to stop whining,
      get off my butt,
      get over it,
      and get the stupid recording
      done.

      Then to Juan
      because I don't want to hear what I suspect,
      that he's finished recording

and submitting
and just waiting for me to say *when*
for our world premiere party.

I stuff my phone in my pocket,
turned off,
because I suddenly know what I need to do.

I take the stairs two at a time
and burst into Davy's room
where I have to yell to be heard
over the Nintendo noise.
Trent adds to the volume with whoops
and shouts every time Mario
bumps Luigi off the track.

"Who's up for going to the park
and then, if all goes well,
ice cream?"

They both throw down the
controls and head for the door
when I remember I haven't checked with Mom,

but

when I see her start to tear up,
I know I've made the right decision
and I also know if I stay one more minute
I'll join her with tears.

We alternately walk
and race
once we get to the park's entrance
just two blocks from our house.
It's always been like an extension to our backyard
and probably the single biggest reason

Mom and Dad chose this house.

I push both boys high
on the swings.
They have the usual contest
to see who can pump even higher.

I spot for Davy while he climbs a spiral ladder
to get up to the platform
that has several choices of slides,
and I watch warily to make sure
he chooses a slide and not the edge.

I watch agile Trent
out of the corner of my eye
as he nimbly swings by his arms
from bar to bar across an elevated climber
and scrambles down the ladder
to run to the other side
and do it all over again.

This is how it should be,
always.

I linger in the moment
even as we head for ice cream at *Ben & Jerry's*
next to the park.

We take our time strolling back,
      dripping,
      slurping,
      gently guiding Davy
      along the sidewalk

when I notice Trent,
      ever so slightly
      hesitate at the curb,

groping with his foot
more than once.

I won't let myself think,
        even for a nanosecond,
that it was anything more
than a bumpy sidewalk
and the distraction
of an ice cream cone.

NOT TO WORRY

Dad grabs the boys for haircuts
and corrals them into the car
while Mom gives me an unexpected hug.

"Thanks, Claire."

I hug her back and break away
before either of us says words
we are both thinking.

It's new, giving me "thank-you" hugs
for paying attention to my brothers.
I grab a cold soda out of the fridge
and plop down on a bar stool next to her.
It's new for me to give them unsolicited attention
        on a Saturday afternoon.

"Ready for the deadline this week?"
Mom's voice comes out almost comical
in its attempt to sound
        casual,
        perky,
        relaxed,
        unworried,

not exhausted,
confident about anyone
or anything.

I give her a long look,
unsure myself
if she really wants to know
or is just making conversation.

"No."

"But you will be, I'm sure."

"Not sure. Not sure at all. I can't
concentrate, and Mom,
when
will we know
about
the blood tests?"

Her hand shakes as she sets her cup down.
"It might be three weeks or so. I'm sorry,
I should have told you..."

not to worry?

I shove the observation
of Trent deep down somewhere
out of sight
where no one can add it
to the

not to worry.

MONDAY PRACTICE ROOM, TEXT TO JUAN

You've submitted, right?

    Not telling.

Why?

    Keep working.

Why?

    Don't want to do this alone.

Why?

    You started it.

Why?

    Good question.

KEEP WORKING!!

I hit 'record,'
get all the way through,
but it's not good
and I know

why.

MONDAY NIGHT, TEXT TO MIA

Wasting my time.

    Why?

Can't concentrate.

    Why?

You know why.

    Excuses.

Tell me I'm whining.

    Why?

Gives me incentive.

    Why?

Always worked before.

    STOP WHINING!!

Smh. One more try tomorrow.

INTERRUPTED CONVERSATION WITH MY FINGERS

Was Dad right about you,
    that playing the piano
    is your destiny,
    our destiny,

and if so

would that translate into
times like these

when no amount of concentration
seems to cut it?

And what kind of future would that be,
so rattled by the distractions
that you can't
> *think,*
> *perform,*
> *function?*

tap—tap—tap

Tara swings the door open
and steps right in
as if invited.

"HE'S NOT HERE,"
I yell in her face.

She jerks away
as if I had just hurled
a flaming torch at her.

"I didn't think he *was*, C l a i r e,"
she says, purring like a hurt kitten,
"but I was just wondering,
um,
who you were talking to?"

"M Y S E L F, Tara,
NOW SHUT THE DOOR,
please?"

And with that I hit 'record,'
soar through "The Kite"
like I've never done before,
listen back

and know I've nailed it.

CREDIT WHERE CREDIT IS DUE

"It is finished," I announce to the world,
        my world, Juan and Mia, at lunch
with the first big grin I've felt like sharing
in several weeks.

"Sounds religious," Mia says
with her impish smile,
"but I think it's more like
musical. See! Getting on your
case about whining did the trick."

She hi-fives me.

Juan puts his sandwich down
to join in.
"Seriously, is it finished and on its way?"
His grin is big, too
and gorgeous.

I grab my cell and scroll through my photos
to find the one Mom took of me
yesterday after school,
        one day ahead of deadline
        at the computer, ready to press "send"
        on the digital copy
        and the scanned, handwritten score.

"I'm proud of you for hanging in there
Claire, in spite of all the stuff
going on in your family. Besides,
like I said,
this was your idea. I'm just playing
follow the leader."

"While we're on the subject,"
Mia says, mouth half-full,
"I hope you both know
it's like
may the best man win here.
I'm impartially partial
to both of you."

Juan flashes the smile
directly across the table
at me
and though I return it,
I know we have that hurdle
yet to cross.
I choose not to let it spoil
the warmth that floats across
right now.

Juan deadpans news-reporter seriousness.
"Yes, and Claire, tell us in your own words,
what finally helped you dig in
and block out the distractions?"

"Oh, that's an easy one, you guys.
No offense to either of you
for your wonderful cheering-on

but

hands down

I owe it all to Tara,
queen of the cheerers-on."

Now *they* exchange quizzical glances
then uproarious laughter
when I describe her visit
to the practice room.

THE LAUGHTER DIES

Juan and I agree at the lockers
that Mia needs to come
to our world premiere popcorn party.
He offers his house,
I offer the popcorn and drinks
and we settle on tomorrow night.

I text Mia from the backseat
while Carlos takes the curves
too fast.
Tara's not in the car to show off for
so I wonder what's up.
I figure Carlos must have a hot date
for the football game.

I open the window and close my eyes,
letting in a delicious whiff
of October air
tinged with decaying leaves
and a hint of smoke.
   The deadline behind me,
    the "premiere party" ahead of me,
for an instant
    I forget the present,
     blotched with blood samples
     and a devastating diagnosis.

"Wake up Claire, I think this is where you live."
Carlos chortles.

"Not asleep, just enjoying the ride,
well, except for being thrown
dangerously about
in the back seat
by the driver's swerves."

"He's in a hurry, Claire. He's gotta get home
and primp up for his date with *Tahrah Tahrah.*"

Carlos reaches across the seat
to hook his brother's neck
in his huge hand.

Juan ducks.

"It all makes perfect sense, now,"
I say, laughing as I climb out
the back seat. I wave goodbye,
and chuckle all the way
to the front door

where

inside,

the laughter quickly dies.

IT'S ALL RELATIVE

Mom perches on her favorite stool
stirring a cup of tea.
She jumps up when she hears me.

She looks older than she was
at breakfast this morning.
I brace myself.

The lab report?
How much worse can it be?
I don't want to hear this.

"A terrible seizure at school.
Bit his lip going down.
Had to have stitches.
Scared the teacher's assistant to death.
She's the one who saw it.
Scared himself.
Thank God he didn't crack his head open.
I just don't know..."

I feel relieved
because this is bad enough
but not the bad
that I thought I was going to hear.

Then guilt
because it's all bad.
Mom looks like death itself
and this is just the beginning.

How will any of us
make it through this terrible nightmare?

I just don't know...

THE PREMIERE

When Dad drops me off at Juan's
for our premiere party

he tells me he's proud of me,

forging ahead with the contest
in the middle of all the mayhem
at home.

It takes me by surprise.
I tell him so
and then *he* looks
surprised.

"Honey, I'm sorry
if I sent the wrong message.
Sometimes dads let their own
issues get in the way. Forgive me?"

I do,
and if my head wasn't already
so full of issues
I would ask what his are.
Instead,
I shrug it off and head for a fun evening.

Juan's mom gives me a hug,
takes the goodies out of my hands,
and says Juan and Mia are waiting
downstairs in what they call
the entertainment area of their modest
split-level.
It's where everything musical happens,
complete with a piano, Carlos's drums,
Juan's flute, recording equipment,
and piles of sheet music and books.

I feel the same nervous tension
that precedes a performance
even though I know it is just the three of us.

I'm glad we decided to include Mia
    but for a split second my mangled brain
    flashes craziness.
    Why did she get here before me?
    What went on before I arrived?

I shake it off as absurdity.

Somehow
the thought of being alone with Juan
lately
sets off a whole new bag of feelings
that I'm not sure I can deal with
right now.

Mia sits on the couch
with a bowl full of popcorn
and the wide-eyed wonderment of a kid
who is bursting at the seams
to see the sequel to a favorite movie.
"Okay, who goes first?
I haven't been to too many
world premieres before
but I gotta tell ya,
I am psyched for this one.
Bring it on."
She takes a big slurp of her soda
and dives back into the popcorn.

Juan looks at me,
sweeps the air with his outstretched arm
and says, "ladies first."

I'm secretly glad to go first
because I am
      ridiculously,
      unbelievably,

uncharacteristically,
nervous.

I go through the usual routine
of settling onto the bench:
      breathing,
      finger flexes,
      focus,

and then

fly "The Kite"
almost flawlessly
for my friends.
They don't catch the few flubs I make
and both jump up with genuine applause
and admiration.

I sigh in relief,

thank them,
and head for the popcorn bowl.

Juan blows some warm air into his flute
as I settle on the couch next to Mia.
Now I am the excited kid
waiting in anticipation.

Juan calls his piece "Present Tense."
I close my eyes,
glad that this gifted friend,
      before he even starts playing,
has given us the opening
to stay totally
in the moment.

It's a jazz piece,

something I expected based on Juan's taste,
and I'm sure it is the most awesome
few minutes I've spent
in months.

I push back tears
again, they'd both think I've flipped,
because of beautiful music
and friends
and mostly because of

the present tense.

LIFE AFTER DEADLINE

Monday morning I wake up with a jolt
to see light where it's usually dark.
     Bacon,
     Nintendo sounds,
     arguing brothers,
     whistling Dad,
     humming Mom,
now I remember. It's a teacher workday
that always falls on Columbus Day,
that always means a vacation day.

I lie back down, remembering.

"The Kite" is on its way;
     out of my control.

Blood test results not back yet;
     out of my control.

The regular routine in our family is
     out of my control.

This
day
is
usually
a
family
day

but I have other plans.

Hunger
and relief from the contest deadline
move my feet down the stairs
in a light-footed
        but cautious patter.

FAMILY DYNAMICS

"There you are, sleepy head."

The airiness in Mom's voice sounds genuine
as she pours more batter on the waffle iron.

Dad checks his watch and deadpans,
"Aren't you late for the practice room, Missy?"

I smile at his wink.

"Sleepy head, sleepy head, sleepy head,"
Davy and Trent chant, parading into the kitchen
and circling me, ready to play tag around me
before I grab Davy in a gentle neck lock,
causing Trent to bump into us and collapse on the floor
in a heap of giggles.

"Hurry up and eat so we can get going."

Davy takes my arm and ushers me to the table.
The reversal of roles sends shivers down my spine.

Mom serves a plate of steaming waffles and bacon
and I dig in,
wondering what the plan is,
buying time to think how I
      should,
      could,
      might
react today

compared to

before.

"What's the plan, Mom?"
I ask, trying to sound casual
after a huge gulp of milk.
I feel less casual when I see *the glance*
pass between my parents.

"Nature Museum, Nature Museum."
Davy and Trent take up the chanting again
until Mom lures them out of the kitchen
with ten more minutes of Nintendo.

Dad says he's sure they told me,
but he's not surprised it got lost in
      the pressure of the past week.

I say Mia has asked me to go with her
to interview Mrs. Shepherd for the school paper
and then hang out
      at the mall for a while.

Mom says at the sink with her back to us,

"Family time is more important now
       than ever."

The waffles threaten to come back up
in the dead silence of a room
where a stealthy beast lurks to steal
all the oxygen.

Dad says I deserve the day off.
Mom says nothing.
I leave the room feeling ugly
       and sure of only one thing.

Batten has rearranged our family
like pieces of familiar furniture
placed awkwardly in a new setting.

DAY-MARE

Mom doesn't hold grudges.
She hollers up the stairs,
     "Enjoy the day.
       Be home by dinner."
She ushers the boys out the door
in a rush of carefree banter
followed by a "See you, hon" from Dad.

I try to figure out what just happened.
Everyone seems fine
but me.

I sit on the side of my bed.
     Sad,
     confused,
     unsure what to do
     with this new feeling:

guilt.

I hurry to get dressed
so I'll be ready when Mia's mom honks.

Maybe
I can shake off the heaviness
that has come over me
        like a day-mare,
        where Davy's life
        depends on my carrying him piggy-back
        over a dank, murky swamp.

REGRETS

When I jump into the back seat
Mia, in the middle of practicing the interview
with her mom,

briefly interrupts to say "hey"
then resumes her professional Katie Couric voice:

"So Mrs. Shepherd, to what do you attribute
your longevity, as you approach your hundredth birthday?"

and

"What do you think is the most amazing invention
during your lifetime?"

and

"Do you have any regrets? Would you have done anything
differently
if you had it to do over?"

Mia's mom shoots back answers
as Mrs. Shepherd
but pauses at the last one.

"Don't you think, Mia dear,
that this one might be a little too
personal? Maybe Mrs. Shepherd does
have regrets that, well,
might be too hard to talk about."

"I don't know," Mia says,
"what does the quiet one
in the back seat think?"

Mia looks over her shoulder
and I realize she's talking to me,
but all I hear is

regrets

and all I know is

you don't have to live to be one hundred
to have them.

A CENTENARIAN'S POV

Mrs. Shepherd lives in a tiny, rundown house
on the edge of a neighborhood in transition.
Mia, with her nose for news,
says it's all about gentrification
and there's another story here
she will surely feature
someday.

After introductions

and repeating slowly
more than once
that I'm just along for the ride,
I try to become invisible
while Mia does her thing.

I marvel at her social skills,
       the easy way with people,
       especially people who are different
       or mega-something
       like Mrs. Shepherd is so mega-old;

and her writing skills,
       editor of the yearbook,
       editor of the school paper;

and the fact that she still hangs out with me,
       the nerd on the fringe
       when anytime she chooses, she could join
       the elites,
       the intellectuals,
       the preps.

I drift in and out of focus,
enjoying the low-intensity day
       when I hear the regret question
       roll out of Mia's mouth
       easy-peasy,
              as we used to say in grade-school.

I hold my breath for a minute,
wondering what kind of response,
       if any,
Mrs. Shepherd will give.
I shift awkwardly in my seat
while Mia looks like she just aced a quiz
everyone else has bombed.

A long silence
and Mia doesn't flinch.

Finally, and almost inaudibly,
Mrs. Shepherd says,

"I didn't celebrate enough."

I cough to stifle a giggle.
What? Are we talking to
an old-time party girl here?

Mia perks up like a bloodhound
and perches her hands expectantly
over her computer keys.

Mrs. Shepherd begins.
"Both my children,
daughter and son
and then my husband,
all taken way before their time
and I mourned,
            Lordy did I mourn,
'til I was no good to no one,
a listless pile of rags
tossed in a heap.
I was useless
and it didn't do them no good now,
did it?
Died and gone to heaven,
I know that for sure,
all of them,
and all my mournin' didn't do
a lick of good.
No sir,
I should have celebrated
their lives,

each one.
I should have *celebrated*."

Mrs. Shepherd slumps down in her chair.
Mia and I jump up
both thinking the worst.

"I'm right tired now, Missies.
Next time, next time you come
I'll show pictures."

Mia takes the cue.
We say good-bye
and quietly slip out
as if leaving church
before the service is over.

ONLY GOOD LEFTOVERS

When I see I've beat them home
I check the kitchen
        out of habit
        and find a note,
"plz put leftover meatloaf in oven."

I settle at the piano,
let Pachelbel's Canon in D
carry my thoughts
        of hundred-year-old ladies celebrating life,
        of brothers celebrating nature,
        of friends celebrating music,
        of parents celebrating family,

when Davy bursts into the house
        followed by Trent, Mom, and Dad.
He slides onto the bench next to me.

I let my fingers finish the piece,
and then lift Davy's fingers onto the keys
to make music,
　　　striking away
　　　any leftover guilt
　　　from this day.

AFRAID

I help clean up after dinner,
glad to hear Mom talk about their day
　　　without putting a negative spin
　　　on my absence—
Davy making friends with a donkey
at the petting zoo;
Trent proving to be a real snake handler;
the challenge of keeping hands inside
the miniature train
as it wound through the thick forest;
and giving Davy enough visual info
to keep him engaged.

Mom asks about my day
and seems interested
in hearing about Mrs. Shepherd's
thoughts on celebrations.

Then a pause
while her face shifts
from relaxed to taut
and I wonder if I am in for it
yet.

"Claire?"

"Yes, Mom?"

"Have you seen anything,
        anything at all
alarming...
no,
not alarming
just...I don't know,
unusual,
maybe out of the ordinary
with...with Trent
lately?"

She looks down
and watches her fingers
twist a tissue
in shaking hands.

I'm afraid she's going to cry.

I'm afraid I know what she's talking about.

I'm afraid to answer

        (*faltering feet on a curb*)

because surely
my imagination
has gotten the best of me.

COMFORT ZONE

I'm glad for Tuesday
        after a holiday.
It always feels like Monday.

I'm even glad for Tara's chatter
in the car

and curiously amused

to hear her tell all
(well, probably not all)
about her date with Carlos
while he obviously struggles
to keep the car on the road.

Juan and I struggle to hold a straight face.
When we get out of the car
we have our usual hearty laugh,
and that carries me through the morning classes
where I refuse
to let images of Trent
      break through,
      break down,
      break into my thoughts.

I'm glad for the lunch chatter
where Mia tells Juan
excitedly
about Mrs. Shepherd
and then asks again
why I don't *ever* contribute
to the school newspaper.

Juan reminds me
we need to get going
on Jazz Night *now,*
      the piece I'll accompany him on.

"Whoa, cut me some slack, friends,"
I say, half mocking, half serious.

"You two are stretching me way beyond my comfort zone
today."

Two faces,

Trent's

and

Davy's,

float into my brain.
I nearly choke on my own words.

*What right do I have
to any comfort zone at all?*

BE GONE

"What's going on?"
Juan asks as we walk to
the music wing after lunch.

I give him a sharp, puzzled look
and wonder
again
how he manages to pick up my vibes
with such spot-on accuracy
like some kind of streaming data nerd.

"What do you mean?" I ask,
knowing exactly what he means
but wanting to hear it from him.

"You are a thousand miles away today,
and Jazz Night doesn't seem

to be on your radar.
More bad news
or no news at all?"

I realize as the question rolls out
that both options
have me in a strangle-hold.
Mentioning what I thought I saw with Trent
seems like a bad omen,

and the blood tests
lurk like a brooding storm.

"A little of both
and nothing I want to talk about
today. Are you cool with that?"

Juan,
always cool
with everything,

smiles and nods
and presses on in his
irresistible way.

"I'll bring your accompaniment
tomorrow so you can get started on it.

Saturday afternoon
at my house,
the first run through?"

I return his smile with a chuckle.

"Sure, Juan
comfort zone be gone."

WRITING ASSIGNMENT

Mia can hardly contain her excitement
over the assignment we just got handed
as we stroll out the classroom door
in Honors English.

Write a narrative to develop real
or imagined experiences or events...

"Of course I'll use Mrs. Shepherd
and get extra mileage out of
the interview. Whoot! Whoot!
Life is goooooood!
What about you, Claire?
Any ideas?"

"Well, I was thinking of
the life and times of a talking piano,
you know, one that converses
with the player's fingers
and together
they plot to take over the world
and make everyone speak in
staccato notes and arpeggios."

She looks at me
dumbfounded
with her bottom jaw dropped.

"Seriously? Did you just think that up
like now, on the spot?"

"Yeah, I sort of did," I say,
savoring her reaction.

"Claire, if you don't start sending me stuff

for "The Chanticleer" soon
I'll... I'll..."

"Be forced to start a "fugue" with me?
Get it? Fugue? Feud? Like ha, ha?"

She shakes her head
in mock disgust
and tells me I've been hangin'
with Juan too much.

Hmm. Too much or not enough?

HEAVY NEWS

I shuffle through the mail
knowing it's way too early
for contest results

but not too early to wonder,
and hope,
and dream,

when

a thick envelope with mysterious
initials,
          BDSRA,
in the return
sends twitches through my fingers.

I want to rip it open,
but it's addressed to my parents
and it feels so heavy...

weighed down

with news
that feels

way
too
heavy.

THE TREE AND THE LEAVES

Juan's jazz piece
stares at me,
speaks to me,
  I dare you
as I slide onto the piano bench
to grab the few minutes
of quiet
before everyone gets home.

A sight-read,
  a second run through,
  and on the third try

I picture dazzling autumn leaves,
all shades of yellow, red, auburn
swirling in an October vortex.
  Untamed,
  playful,
  relentless,
  free spirited,
around a bare-branched,
unbending,
mediocre
tree.

My fingers laugh in my face.

Who said jazz isn't fun?

Can you guess who is the tree
and who the leaves?

MISSING INFORMATION

The wind whipping around the tree
outside my window
wakes me up,
and I snuggle back under the covers.

It's Saturday

and I chuckle, remembering that
the leaves and I
have a practice date this afternoon.
I wonder what Juan would think
if I told him about the mental picture,
   tree with dancing leaves,
that pops up when my classical fingers
try to let go,
   jazz-like,
on the accompaniment
while he rips it up
with some kind of awesome
and the slightest bit of effort
on the flute.

The brother-noise downstairs
reminds me it's been a quiet week.
  No seizures,
  no news,
  nothing out of the *new* ordinary.

I decide to join the mayhem in the kitchen

and grab the last two pancakes
while Trent shows Davy
the running-back play
he learned in flag football this week.

I stop eating and watch.

Way awesome for a six-year-old.
Way too awesome.

Mom stops loading the dishwasher
        like a paused video.
Dad puts his cup down and freezes.
I become aware that my parents are
        not just watching my brothers
        but studying them,
        looking beyond the football moves

as if an important piece of a puzzle
were floating somewhere in
the chaos.

HUG

After we finish practicing
I tell Juan about the tree
and the leaves.
He dances around the room,
        around me—the tree—
waving his flute
like a magic wand,
arms flourishing,
feet doing crazy Michael Jackson moves
until we are both in hysterics.

"About time I see you laugh again," he says,

collapsing on the floor.

It catches me off guard
and I remember I'm talking to
my oldest and most trusted friend
besides Mia.

"It's been so quiet all week
but my parents..."

"You got the blood test results?"

"No, but that's just it. It's the same
stupid tension,
unspoken,
that we had before we found out,
        you know,
about Davy.
And you should have seen them this morning
watching the boys while they played,
watching them,
watching Trent, really
looking for symptoms, I think.
That's it.
I really think they expect the worst."

"Do you, Claire?"

I can't hold back the tears
and I tell him in huge, blubbering gasps
about what I've seen
and what my mother has seen.

He pulls me towards him
and hugs me tight
while I cry it out.

LOOKS

Mia catches up with me
on our way to Honors English.

"So, are you sticking with the
magic piano story or has the musician
        with no ideas
come up with another doozy?"

"Fresh out of doozies, I'm afraid,
so it'll have to be the talking piano.
This musician with no ideas
is knee deep in jazz practice
with Juan and..."

"Juan, hmmm?"
Mia says, giving me her best
Cruella DeVille look.

"Yeah, you know,
our friend from Kindergarten,
and why are you looking at me
that way, My-yah Me-yah?"

"Speaking of looking,
have you noticed the way
he's been looking at *you*
lately?"

No.
I mean maybe
and after I savor it a while,
I'll tell you
what I noticed
about his hug.

Winter Part 1

THE BEAST

Juan glances at me over his shoulder
with concern
when Carlos pulls into the driveway
behind both cars.

Both cars are never in the driveway
at this time of day.

"Want us to wait?
        Want us to come in?
        What would you like us to do,
        Claire?"

Tell me this is going to be alright.

"Nothing, thanks.
I'll text you."

I hop out of the car fast
but my feet drag like lead
all the way to the door.

They both stand up
when I come in
like in old-time movies
when gentlemen stand
for a lady entering a room.

Mom lets some papers she's holding
slide to the floor
as she stands
and moves to embrace me.
Dad joins the hug
and then the tears
and no one needs to say a word

because the beast,
the monster,
Batten
is loose in the room,
in our family
not once,
but twice
and a half.

THE DETAILS

We move to the couch in a cluster
as if one of us would fall
if we didn't all hold on.

The first thing I think,
looking toward the door,
is that Davy is going to burst in
any minute
until Mom says she arranged a play date
for both of them.

Dad blows his nose and collects himself
enough to begin
with more details than I can absorb,
than I want to absorb,
but it's something he needs to do
so I listen numbly.

Davy and Trent both have juvenile Batten,
the most common of a group of disorders called
neuronal ceroid lipofuscinoses.

I want to scream.

It's rare.

Maybe two to four of every hundred thousand live births
in the US are affected.

It's an autosomal recessive disorder.
        You get it only if you inherit
        two copies of the defective gene
        like Davy and Trent did,
        one from each parent.

I don't want to hear this.

Dad looks at Mom as if he wants to die.
He says he and she both carry one defective gene.
That means
each of their children faces a one-in-four chance
of developing Batten

or a one-in-two chance
of inheriting just one copy of the gene,
making them a carrier.

I jump up and pace in front of him,
out of control, sobbing.

"Tell me, Dad, am I doomed, too?
Is that why we are here right now?
Are you going to tell me it's three out of three?"

He stands,
grabs me into his arms,
shaking me like a naughty child,
nearly shouting back

"NO   NO   NO!
I should have told you
right at the beginning.
It usually strikes children

between five and eight
and Claire, of course you don't have it
but..."

Mom jumps up and joins us again,
speaking almost in a whisper.

"Honey...you,"

       deep breath

"you
are
a
carrier."

CARRIER

My head throbs,
swirling inside
as if my own mother
had just hit me in the gut
and stands watching, waiting for me
to collapse.

I shake loose from the cluster of three
and stagger back to the couch.

What does that mean,
      what she just said?
         Carrier?
What does that mean?

I put my head in my hands
seriously feeling faint now,
nauseous,

miles away as if I had just stepped
       out
of my own body.

Is it relief that I'm experiencing
or terror
because of the blank hole this information
has burned in my brain?

"I…I don't understand
what it means
being a carrier."
I force the words out
trying to beat down the waves of nausea.

Mom sits down next to me,
takes both hands in hers,
and looks squarely into my eyes.

"It simply means, Claire,
that you can pass the mutated gene
on to your own children
one day,

but it's not something
you need to think about
right now.
       Certainly not
          right now."

Good.
I won't.
I can't.
I don't want to
think about it
ever.

THE QUESTIONS

They ask me if I have any other questions
before Dad leaves to pick up my brothers,
     my desperately ill,
      terminally ill brothers.
I shake my head.
"I need to be alone."

Once inside my room I lock the door and pace
until I collapse onto my bed, bury my face
in the pillow, and let the sobs come in muffled waves.

Anger
    How could this happen to our family,
    to my precious little brothers?
    How can I live a normal life
    and watch them die?

Guilt
    Why did I win the luck of the draw?
    Why do I get to live and they don't?
    Where was my concern for Trent
        in the conversation just now?

Fear
    How will I plan for my own family
      someday
      with this ghost,
      this beast
        in my genes?

Frustration
    Can't somebody
    DO SOMETHING
      to stop this from happening?

THE UNDERSTUDIES

Mom taps on my door
to say dinner is ready
      but she would understand
      if I want to eat in my room
        alone
          just this once.

It would be easy
      just this once,

like going way around the sighting
of a grizzly bear today

and meeting him for breakfast tomorrow.

"No, just let me splash some water on my face,"
I say,
"so the boys don't...
I mean, so I, you know,
look presentable."

"Thanks, honey."
She leaves before the courage
in the room evaporates.

It's as if they've been practicing this role
like understudies for years
and now
it's time for the big performance
and they are in perfect form.

Mom asks Davy how his play date was,
her voice as bright and chirpy
as breakfast on Christmas morning.

Trent jumps in to tell Davy,
        more than the rest of us,
how his friend, Sam,
thinks he knows how to play flag football
but really
he doesn't because every time he gets the ball
he fumbles.

As if on cue, right after the blessing, Dad says,
"Okay boys, picture the piano, right?"

They zoom in on Dad,
        an eye-sparkling audience
when he's about to tell a joke,
like he's about to pull a rabbit out of a hat.

"Listen up now, there might be a reward
for the one who gets this. Ready?"

Davy pipes up, "How about extra dessert?"

Dad feigns shock, then deep thought
and an evil smile, "Veel see about dat."

He continues in full accent,
"Vi eez de peeahno zo 'ard to opeeen?"

Mom tells the boys to keep eating
while they think
and my muddled brain *tries* to think
while I push food around the plate,
knowing for sure I can't eat.
I doubt I would come up with an answer today,
even though I've heard it before.

I stare at Trent's curly blonde hair
and beautiful blue eyes,

how they light up when he's having fun,
like right now.
     How long will it be
     before that light goes out?

I look across the table at Davy,
at the constant smile he wears on his face.
     Will that smile follow him
     all the way to the end?

Davy and Trent toss answers around the table:
     Because it's locked.
     Because it's stuck.
     Because it's broken.
     Because the player is too dumb.

We all smile at the last one

and when the boys give up,
we all groan at the answer,
"because the keys are on the inside."

"Okay, okay, the cat got that one
but you should be able to get this next one
based on what you just learned.
Listen up, now.
Where did the music teacher leave his keys?"

Dead silence, and some chewing and slurping
then Trent blurts out, "On the piano!"

Mom and Dad keep up the act
while I fight back tears.

He's so darned bright.

WITH JUAN'S HELP

It's after midnight
when I fall into bed,
sure that I will never again
     simply fall asleep.

I remember the promise to text Juan.
I decide it's too late
when I see an 11:45 message from him.

     R u ok?
I start
and stop
and start again.

     Idk.
     Me half…Trent all.
     Why why why?
     Can't live with this.
     Can't.
     CAN'T!!

I'm sobbing again
ready to throw the phone
and scream into the pillow.

Juan responds.

     Sooooo bummed.
     So damn bummed.
     I could come over.

Finally thinking of someone but myself…

     NO TY.
     Parents in bed.

> C u tomorrow.

And just as I turn out the light,
Juan's words:

> U can.
> U will.
> I'll help.

Better than a sleeping pill.

THE STALKER

For once I'm glad it's Tuesday
and even more relieved when
Carlos and Tara carry on
with puppy-love banter
ad nauseam.
If Juan tipped them off to keep it light
before I got in,
their script is priceless.

Juan glances over the seat
with a look almost painfully
compassionate,
but I return it with gratitude...
        no, something way beyond gratitude
and a weak but thankful smile.

Our walk to the lockers,
        the time usually spent giggling
        over the car conversation,
turns awkward.

"Juan, about last night..."

"Honest, Claire, we don't have to talk about it yet if..."

"No, I mean, your offer to help..."

"Well, sure, whatever I can do, I mean..."

"Thanks. Just...thanks."

He sees the tears coming
and oddly
quickens his pace

while I don't cry
and oddly
wonder why
I'm disappointed he didn't hug me.

I feel the beast stalking me
like a new predator
lurking around familiar territory—
        my turf,
        my solid ground,
causing tiny seismic tremors
that threaten to open the earth
and devour me
and all that matters to me.

QUIET DAY

I slog through the day
like a robot
relying on some kind of pre-programming
to deliver me from class to class—
        feet moving without navigating,
        eyes looking without seeing,
        brain receiving without processing.

I don't question the wide berth
I'm getting from teachers and friends
or the fact that Juan and Mia
appear by my side
like angels shadowing me
periodically
throughout the day.

Juan must have put out an all-points bulletin:
    She's fragile as glass today because...

It got me through the day
but packing up after the last bell,
I'm feeling isolated
and exhausted.

As if they picked up my signal,
Juan and Mia swoop down on me
from both sides,
each grabbing an arm.

"C'mon, we heard Schmoozies calling,
and we decided we would let you tag along,"
Mia says, working hard to keep it light
and playful.

I start to resist when Juan puts his hand up
like a good traffic cop
and offers me his arm
like a good escort
and beams a broad smile
like the good friend he is.

I let him lead me out the door
where the sharp blast of November wind
feels good to my dulled senses
on the two-block walk

to everybody's favorite hangout,
    but what feels even better
    is the way Juan knows
    when to let me be
    quiet.

SCHMOOZIES

The near capacity after-school noise—
    loud chatter,
    dish clatter and bang,
    chair scrapes—
jarring at first
and then suddenly welcome,
like waking up out of a disturbing dream,
    relieved to know
    you are alive.

For the first time all day
I actually form a thought:
    yes, I am alive

and then

    should I be?

We head for the table in the back,
our usual spot, spilling over with
    Tara and Carlos,
    Mia and her off-again, on-again friend Kyle,
    Juan and me.

Finally I feel like talking
as I look around the table at my friends.
"If I didn't know better
I'd say someone has called a meeting, guys."

It breaks the tension and Mia jumps in.
"We just want you to know we're here for ya, Claire,
whatever we can do to help..."

They nod, smile, and murmur in agreement.
I'm thankful the walk over
chased away potential tears.

There's so much that I want to say, like
how much I don't know
about the disease,

and

how I don't deserve to live
while my little brothers are going to die,

and

how I feel so scared,

and

how the future—
        theirs
        and mine—
is so shrouded in a black cloud
of uncertainty,

but

for now I welcome the warmth
of friendship
on a cold November day.

JUST A BAD DREAM

It's almost midnight.
Today's homework sits
      unfinished
      on my desk.
Scattered, disorganized papers
glare at me, dare me
to get on with the program,
the business of life.

The ticking clock on my wall
a noisy gong, reminding me
that time has a new meaning
in our family.

The quiet house
whispers a lie that all is well
at the end of the day.

My restless, wide-awake eyes
dart from the half-finished narrative,
      "The Life and Times of the Talking Piano,"
      burdened, weighed down by eraser marks,
to the desk calendar,
red-lettered events that jump out like hazard signs now—
      Jazz Night.
      Thanksgiving.
      Christmas vacation begins here.

Thump! Bump!

My heart lurches at the sounds
outside my door
and I jump up, nearly knocking down Trent,
looking dazed,

rubbing his eyes
and beginning to cry.

"Come here, buddy," I say,
pulling him onto my lap.
"Having a bad dream?"

"Um...hmmm."

I hold him,
          rock him in my arms like Mom would do
until he falls back asleep,
and I crawl into my own bed
          shaking,
               cold to the bone.
I pull the covers over my head
wishing with all my might
that it was
just
a
bad
dream.

BIG FAT 'D'

I slide into my seat in Honors English
to the sound of rustling papers,
murmuring voices,
as the narratives are being returned.

I quickly grab mine
while Mia flashes her
'A+' across the aisle,
          the one about Mrs. Shepherd,
before she can see the 'D'
at the top of my paper,

the one about the talking piano
and scribbled teacher notes
in red: *Claire, please see me.*

The large red 'D' reverberates
in my head where images
of Davy flash alternately
with Trent

and 'd' words,
          disease,
          diagnosis,
          death,
swirl like a dust storm,
          disgusting,
          disturbing,
          dreadful,
          demonic,

and then

          deserving.

Maybe I deserve this 'D'
because I didn't really try,
          didn't really care,
to do anything but feel sorry for myself
last week.

Maybe I
          don't deserve to live
while my two innocent brothers
          die.

LET IT OUT

"Not good, huh Claire?"

Mia catches up with me
on the way out the door.

"Dumb," I mutter.

"You? Get real."

"Yeah, well, I just spent
some creative brainstorming
coming up with 'd' words
and I forgot 'dumb.' I knew
the talking piano was a
dumb idea."

"And I knew it was an awesome idea,
but give yourself a break. Look at
what's going on in your life right now."

It isn't Mia's fault that I can no longer hold in
the tears that have been building,
not just this day
but for the past week,
trying to live life as it once was
when everything has turned upside down.

Mia looks apologetic,
somehow responsible for this flood
as she puts her arm over my shoulders
and ushers me into the nearest bathroom.
She grabs my book bag
and we both slide down the cold tile wall
where she holds me like a mother
while my sobs echo

around the empty bathroom.

"It's not the 'D' you know..."

"For sure," Mia says,
handing me a wad of tissue.
She stays silent in her
motherly role as the tears subside.

"It's just that I feel
so guilty for living,
for even being alive,
for knowing that I will
live, live, live
to watch them
die, die, die.
What did they do to deserve to die
so young
and what have I done
to deserve to live
at all?"

Mia is slow to answer.

"I'm no psychologist
you know,
but I think I'd probably
be feeling the same way
if I was in your shoes, Claire.
It's not your fault, but if you're
feeling this way, maybe
you should, like,
go talk to the counselor or
someone who knows about
this stuff, you know?"

I look into Mia's clear green eyes

and I realize I feel like smiling.
"Counselor? No way.
She's an old biddy
and not nearly as effective
as your big shoulder.
I think I just needed to say those
words to someone
and you're the lucky one.
Thanks, friend."

"Anytime, Claire."

We go our separate ways to class
and I replay the conversation.
Something about what just happened feels good,
but I'm not exactly sure why.

TWENTY 'HELPS'

Juan's text message plays in my head
as I dash to meet him in the practice room.

> *U can.*
> *U will.*
> *I'll help.*

help?
help!
help.
helps
may I help you?
please help yourself
help oneself
help out
helping hand
helper

helpmate
helped
helpful
helpfulness
helpfully

helpless
helplessly
helplessness
help is on the way

so help me, God.

We reach the door at the same time
from different directions.

"Tell me what it is, please!"

"What do you mean?" I say,
opening the door
while he stares at me.

"Something about the glazed-over eyes
tells me there's something really rad
going on inside that pretty head."

How does he read me like this?

"I think I'm really going nuts,
that's all."

"Awesome. I want to hear all about it."
He sinks down on the floor cross-legged
and motions for me to follow.
"I mean, not awesome about going nuts
but awesome that you are, well,
back. I've been worried about you."

He's given me the floor—
his total attention,
his friendship,
his ear.

Flustered,
embarrassed,
tongue-tied,
I say, "I just came up with twenty
ways to use the word 'help.'"

The look on his strong, open face
morphs like a cloud in high wind:
        stunned,
                amused,
relieved,
        accepting,
loving.

He grabs my hands and pulls me up, laughing.
"It's time for jazz.
Come on, let's do it!"

PRACTICE

We both warm up with some scales
and without a word,
jump into the first piece.
I feel Juan's patience as I flub
and flounder
the first few times through,
        the first time I have touched a keyboard
in over a week.
I'm sorely aware that under
normal circumstances

I would have mastered my part
long before this first session with Juan.

"Hey, hey. Not bad for a crazy lady."

"You're too kind, maestro."
I search his face for the disappointment
in me
that I feel.
Kindness is what I see.

We stay with it another hour.
I am assured I will be able to deliver,
to accompany my best friend,
back him up while he shines,
thankful that all eyes and ears
will be on him
rather than me.

He swabs his flute out
and I mess with a few strains
of "The Kite."

"Sounds good.
We should be hearing about
the contest soon, right?"

"Yeah, before or after Christmas.
I'm not sure. I forget. Sometime..."

"Hey, don't be drifting back into
la-la land," Juan says, touching my shoulder.
"I like you better
as the crazy lady."

I smile.
"Careful. I might start

a list of words about
you
and then we'll see
who's crazy."

He steps towards me
like he's going to hug me
but he doesn't.
Maybe
like earlier, when I started to talk
but pulled back.

We need more practice.

THE SAME BUT DIFFERENT

Mom bustles around
the kitchen talking to herself
with grocery list in hand.

Dad's at a day-long music workshop.

Davy and Trent are upstairs
giggling, for once not arguing
over a Nintendo move.

I put the finishing touches
on homework and let my thoughts
drift to Juan,
how we seem
        not quite apart
        not quite together.

The background noises in our house
remind me that our family is
        not quite the same,
        but a whole lot different.

And me?

Am I apart or together,
the same or different?

"Claire," Mom's voice
saves me from
questions I can't answer.

"I'm off to the grocery store.
You're in charge and I'll be a while.
It's turkey and trimmings and long lines."

She's out the door
and I gravitate to the piano,
another reminder that some things
are still the same
but a little bit different.
Maybe it's the way the keys feel,
or is it the way I feel about the keys?

I have full twenty-twenty
but I'm a carrier;

  the same,
  but different.

THE ONLY FEARFUL ONE

"Claire, Claire, come quick.
It's Davy."

Trent's voice breaks through
my reverie.

"Work it out, guys," I holler,

thinking their peace had
reached its usual limit.
I go on playing.

"NO! NO! Something's wrong
with Davy. Come now!"

I hear the urgency
and bolt up the stairs,
unprepared for what I see.
Davy is on the floor,
arms flailing,
legs shaking up and down,
body writhing,
while Trent hovers
speechless
in the corner.
Something kicks me out
of fuzziness
and I lean down
to maneuver him
onto his side.
I slide the chair away
from his face,
trying to remember if I should
use my fingers to check for obstructions.
I'm about to call 911
when the tremors begin to subside.
His rigid arms and legs relax
and he opens his eyes,
looking dazed and confused.

I gently lift him up on his bed,
position him on his side,
and watch while his breathing eases
into a deep sleep.

Trent scoots over to sit beside me
on the floor. I concentrate
on slowing my heart rate
and steadying my breathing.
"Do you think we should call Mom?"
Trent's voice quivers as he
pulls in closer.

I cough to test my shaky voice,
not taking my eyes off of Davy.
"Let's just sit here for a while with him.
I think he's okay now.
She'll be home soon."

I look at Davy's peaceful face
and feel Trent's body relax,
snuggling up next to me
with no clue about what lies ahead.

Clearly, the only fearful one
in this room
is
me.

CAR CHATTER

Mia convinces me to come along
for another visit with Mrs. Shepherd.
While driving us there her mom
asks about the boys.
I give a quick answer
minus the seizure day,
still too full of pain
and fear.

I'm glad for Mia's chatter.

"This time take random notes
and who knows what wild idea
you will come up with for your
next paper. That's how it works,
you know."

She has no humility about her
writing prowess,
but her next comment reminds me
that neither do I
about music.

"So aren't you just dying to hear
the contest results? Should be soon,
right? You know I love Juan,
but secretly
I hope it's you."

> What does she mean
> she 'loves' Juan?
> Am I getting paranoid now?

I'm glad she can't see
the blush spread across my face—

> shame for doubting her motives,
> shame because I secretly hope I win, too;

> fear
> that it will screw my friendship with Juan
> if I do.

A GOLDMINE

I swear Mrs. Shepherd looks like
some kind of time-warped little girl.
She's decked out in a bright
blue-flowered dress,
blue eyes sparkling,
the usual bobby sox and
Day-Glo tennis shoes,
and a smile that makes the deep
grooves on her leathery face
seem insignificant.

"Come in, girls,"
she says, patting the couch
on either side of her.
"I've got pictures today,
just like I promised."

I follow Mia's lead
and whip out my notepad.
Mrs. Shepherd dives into the first album,
flipping from page to page
and stopping to comment.

"That's Billy afiddlin'
and Mary keepin' him company,
I always called it.
She was second to none on that keyboard
but in her element makin' him shine.
They were a twosome, always featured
at the school talent shows,
        always together,
        always makin' some kind
        of music."

I want to stop and ask questions

but her voice, the stream of memories,
     is mesmerizing.

I remember what she said
last visit, about not celebrating their lives enough.
It looks to me like
life was one big celebration.
Maybe I'm missing something.
Mia points to a particular picture
that lights Mrs. Shepherd up
like a sparkler on Fourth of July.

"Ah, the hootenanny.
Pete Seeger. Ever heard of him?"

Mia turns to me with a blank stare.

"Of course. Folk music. The sixties.
Your kids must have loved it."

"I took them to see Seeger in New York.
Every week after that, they held
a hootenanny with their friends,
right here in our basement."

She suddenly slumps back on the couch,
     closes her eyes,
and for a few minutes we fear the worst
like last time.

"Even hootenanny memories are too much for old ladies."
She opens her eyes and chuckles.
"Next time, maybe we'll listen to one."

Mia waits until we're in her mother's car
then explodes. "I swear, Claire, if that
wasn't some kind of awesome...

That woman is a goldmine! This series on her life
is going to knock it out of the ballpark
for me and the school paper."

"I can't argue with that, at least
the goldmine part," I say with a wry smile.
My notepad is empty
but my head
and my heart
overflow.

JAZZ NIGHT

The usual pre-concert adrenalin
puts my fingers on alert as we wait
in the wings
for our turn on stage.

It's hard to believe it will be
our third year at this all-school event
with Juan on jazz flute
and me, the piano accompanist.

It's his show
and I'm glad.
We are Mary and Billy
and I'm just keeping him company
as Mrs. Shepherd would say.
The thought gives me chuckles,
evoking a slightly alarmed look from Juan
as we walk on stage.

Juan slides into the opening with ease
and as he weaves through the riffs and trills,
the funky staccato notes running up and down the scales,
I realize how much of Herbie Mann's

"Memphis Underground" has found
a warm spot in my mostly classical heart.

Juan is near the end of this long piece,
a flawless performance that splashes
energy and rhythm across the stage
and into the audience

when suddenly,
I realize with horror
my beat is off, this one part
that I knew needed more practice...

I'm messing this up!
I'm messing Juan up!

I stop playing
and pray that the audience will see it
as a planned solo finale
showcasing Juan.

And Juan? How will he see it?
And me? What is it that I *need* to see?

BROKEN THANKSGIVING

In the past,
the Monday before Thanksgiving
meant a short, light school week
before a long, fun, family weekend.

This Monday morning is like watching
a foreign film without subtitles.

Trent   woke us all up before dawn,
         screaming from a nightmare

that has carried over into an argument
about not wanting to go to school.

Dad   just left early for his first class
after what sounded like an argument
between him and Mom.
He slammed the door hard.

I   screwed up the accompaniment
at Jazz Night Saturday,
causing Juan to have to improvise
the last section of the piece to cover up.

Davy   had a bad seizure right before Jazz Night
so Mom and Dad stayed home.
Maybe that's a good thing
that they stayed home.

Thanksgiving anyone?

Ours is broken
and I have no idea
how to fix it.

KINDNESS AGAIN

I take out my sandwich.
Juan sits down.
He takes out his sandwich.
Mia slides in next to Juan.
She looks at both of us
looking at our sandwiches.
She takes out her sandwich.

"I'm sorry, Juan."

"No, it's okay, Claire."

Mia tracks us like a tennis match.

"It's *not* okay."

"Okay,...then it's *not* okay."

Mia stops chewing and just tracks.

"Davy had a seizure right before we went out the
door."

"You know how sorry I am about that."

Mia quickly cleans up and leaves without a word.

"But I messed up, messed you up, and look what
I did to Jazz Night."

"Yeah, you messed up, and we managed to pull it off
anyway.
But forget Jazz Night. Look what you are doing to
you."

He finally looks straight into my eyes.
It's kindness again.
He's killing me
with his kindness.

WHITE NOISE

I'm glad for noisy cleanup clatter
         after Thanksgiving dinner,
white noise to my grey thoughts.

maybe it's a good thing Gram and Gramps

    couldn't make it this year
but then again
Mom and Dad are doing such a bang-up job
of acting like nothing is wrong
and by the luck of the draw
we had no seizures at the table
or arguments
so maybe Gram and Gramps
    should have come this year
because who knows what
another year will bring

and

maybe Juan is really mad at me
about the Jazz Night mess
but he's too nice to say it
to my face
but then again
I don't understand what he meant by
what I'm doing to myself
and I wonder what happened to his offer
to help

and

maybe Mrs. Shepherd exaggerates too much
because it looks like her kids
were always happy in those pictures
and that seems like celebrating life to me
but then again
maybe she has a dark side
and came down on them a lot
and that wasn't in the pictures

and

"Claire."
Dad's voice interrupts my thoughts
so I almost drop a plate.

"Your mother is taking the boys
to a movie. How about a walk
in the park?"

Dad won't get an Oscar
for his portrayal of casual
and neither will I
for my rendition of carefree.

"Sure, Dad. Be with you
in a sec!"

SMALL TALK IN THE PARK

Dad doesn't do small talk well.
"I know it's been hard on you, honey.
Your mother and I are,
well, we just,
we want to make sure..."

"Dad, get to the point," I snap. "If there's
more bad news just tell me. I can't
stand to hear..."

He stops in his tracks and grabs
me by the shoulders, almost shaking me.
"Claire, listen to me. There's nothing
more that you don't already know,
but I think you can see the way it's
going. Your mother and me,
        you,
            the three of us,

we've got to pull it together.
The boys are doing better
than the three of us.
We've got to be there for them
and, we, I, well I'm not..."

He, my dad, covers his face with his hands
and breaks into sobs
for the second time in my life.
I look around,
        disgusted at myself
        for looking around to see who
        might be watching my father fall apart,
and then steer us to the nearest bench.

I listen to him blow his nose
while I try to decide what makes me angrier:
        his show of weakness,
        the ugly beast,
or
        the expectation I should feel thankful today.

NO MORE BAD NEWS

"Dad, are you and Mom getting a divorce?"

I almost laugh
in relief
at the mortified look on his face.

"Oh Claire, no, no, of course not.
We're solid as a rock,
but rocks get weathered in constant storms
and this is a storm
that's not going to let up.
I'm not handling it so well,

that's what I wanted to say
and, well,
I'm concerned about how you're handling it."

He hugs me tight to his side.
I manage to hold my tears in
but his tears make it easier to talk.

"Yeah, I guess I'm having a hard time, too, Dad.
I messed up at Jazz Night.
It's not like me. I'm...distracted.
Things don't look the same anymore.
Even the keyboard looks different,
no, feels different
like I'm not the same person playing it
or my hands aren't the same hands
as before.
Even my friends feel different."

My thoughts leap to Juan
but I stop short.
It's not something my father would get.

Dad is back to himself.
"Claire, there is an organization
that might be able to help us
get a grip, as you say. They have
a conference in a few weeks and Mom
has volunteered to stay with the boys
while you and I go do some
fact-finding."

He spends the next fifteen minutes
telling me what was in that fat envelope
from BDSRA
that I wondered about earlier.

"But you said yourself there is
no cure. What good would it do
to go to a depressing conference if there is
no hope for a cure?"

He gives me an intense stare.

"I don't know, Claire. I'm grasping
at straws. I'd like you to come
with me and maybe we can find out
together."

I ask if I can think about it.

"Middle of next week?"

I shrug in agreement.
I'm finally thankful for something:
that we got home
from a simple walk
without
any more
bad news.

SCHMOOZIES GROUP THERAPY

I hadn't intended on turning
a casual Schmoozie visit into
a group therapy session,
but that's how it plays out
when I mention how things are so
        uptight
at home
and how my dad thinks he and I
should go to this conference.

Tara chimes in first:
>Yeah, Claire! I've missed hearing you
>in the practice room on my way
>to cheerleading practice.
>Seems like it's been forever.

Carlos follows:
>It's like my wrestling matches, man,
>the more people you meet out there
>the more you know you got it good.

Mia jumps in:
>Oh Claire, it's gotta' be hopeful
>just meeting all those people who are going through
>the same thing.

Kyle looks tongue-tied, but tries:
>Yeah, Claire, I don't know your brothers
>but trying to understand them
>will only help you;
>I know from my mom's bout with cancer.

Juan, grabbing my hand in the crowded booth:
>Finally, Claire. Tara's right.
>Let the music
>come back into your life.

He squeezes my hand
and his clear dark eyes
search deep into mine.
I want to say a thousand things
to him
and I want him to kiss me,
but both will have to wait
for an alone moment...
>maybe the next time
>we share the music together.

INTRODUCTION

It's spitting snow when the cab
lets us out at the Brunswick Hotel
in downtown Cincinnati.
It occurs to me that this isn't
one of those destination cities you hear about
where it's nonstop fun
and then I remember,
we didn't come here to have
any fun at all.

I suddenly feel sick.
        What will we find out?
        What will we not find out?
        Who will we meet?
        Why did I let Dad
            and my friends
            talk me into this?

A large banner draped across the front desk reads
"Welcome Batten Disease Support and Research
Association."
It's the first time I've seen it all written out
and I shiver from the cold wind that blew in behind us
and the icy thoughts invading my brain.

An overly jolly man approaches Dad
as if he recognizes him.
He doesn't, but he introduces himself as Henry
and ushers us to the registration table.

While Dad signs us in
I notice a crowd of people drifting in and out
of a room across the hall,
and I make a mental note to check it out later.

Something lightly bumps the back of my leg
and I turn around to see a girl
in a wheelchair smiling up at me.

...the more people you meet out there
the more you know you got it good...

"I'm sorry," the woman pushing the chair says.
"It looks like we all arrived
at the same time." She smiles, reaches out a hand.
"I'm Sharon and this is Melissa," she says,
patting the girl on the shoulder.
Melissa lifts her hand in a wobbly gesture
but I'm not sure
if she is trying to wave
or waiting to shake my hand
and then I notice
she is blind.
She says "hi" in a gravelly, too-loud voice
and laughs. Her mom reaches down to
wipe the drool from her mouth.
"Hi, Melissa," I say, shoving my hands
awkwardly in my coat pockets.

"Your first time?"
Sharon asks.

"Uh, yeah. I'm here with my dad."

...just meeting all those people
who are going through the same thing....

I don't feel like talking
but I don't want to be rude.
I'm relieved when Dad guides me to another table
without noticing Sharon and Melissa

where we pick up a thick packet of information
and then head to our room.

"Okay, let's see. Looks like there
is a 'general meet and greet' in a few minutes
followed by dinner and a
'new family' orientation."

"Dad, can we cut a deal while we're here?"

"Sure, honey, what is it?"

"Can you stop pretending everything is so,
so, you know, like, normal? I mean,
I saw some people out in the lobby
who look really sick, you know,
and I just don't think it's a good idea
to be all happy and everything
when they are so bad off,
you know what I mean?"

Dad gives me a quizzical look
that I can't exactly read
but he finally smiles,
says "Deal,"
and tells me we have ten minutes
before going downstairs.

...trying to understand them
will only help you...

MEET AND GREET

A room too small
too warm
too congested with

too many wheelchairs, strollers, walkers
holding too many young children
      laughing
           twisting
jerking
      smiling
           drooling
staring
      talking
           living
    dying.

It looks like no one
is having trouble breathing

but
me.

NEW FAMILY ORIENTATION

This room is too chilly
and set up like a meeting room
with rows of chairs.
We come in late and take seats
in the back row.

I see no wheelchairs, only two strollers—
brother and sister, it looks like,
and a girl about my age.

I count six fathers
who shoot up from their chairs
one at a time,
introduce themselves
in strong, superficially confident voices
      like Dad sounded yesterday,

and describe their family members
who have Batten disease,
> some here at the conference,
> some left at home.

Now Dad rises slowly to his feet,
begins to speak
and abruptly chokes up.
Some heads turn,
others look down in their laps.
The man running the meeting
waits patiently while Dad recovers
enough to introduce us
in a voice rife with emotion.

"Thank you, Sam, for bringing us
to where we need to be in this group,
and that is dealing honestly with
the way our lives have changed."

I look up at Dad with admiration
> wishing I could take back a few things
> I've said recently.
I loop my arm through his
and lean in to hug his shoulder.

...where we need to be
> *...where we need to be*

TIPS FOR THE FAMILY

I immediately like
the man at the front of the room.
He keeps a smile on his round, flushed face
and strokes his beard absently
as he talks.

I can feel Dad relax.
I remember to take out the notebook
Mia made me promise to bring.
He's not long into his talk,
        "Tips for the Family,"
before I realize I'm scrambling
to get down every word
as if my life depended on it.
I smile
when I consider that
        maybe,
        just maybe,
the life of our family
does depend on it.

I write (as thoughts race through my head):
take charge of your life
        (yeah, right: out of control)
don't let the disease always take center stage
        (boy do we need help on this one)
quality time for self
        (that means me, too!)
watch out for depression/get help if need to
        (is that what the tears are about?)
accept help/suggest specific needs
        (I need to talk to Juan)
educate selves
        (is this where we start?)
promote loved one's independence
        (Davy at the piano, Trent in sports)
trust instincts
        (mine, or just Mom and Dad's?)
grieve and then dream new dreams
        (really, is it that simple?)
stand up for rights as caregiver and citizen
        (not sure I get this one)

seek support of other caregivers
(well, we're here, aren't we?)

MEMORIAL ROOM

My hand is tired,
my thoughts are flying
        faster than prestissimo,
and a strange kind of energy
pulses clear down to my toes.

I wonder if Mia feels this way
when she comes from one of her
interviews.

"Good for you for taking notes, Claire,"
Dad says, breaking through my buzzing thoughts
with a side hug.
"Maybe you could type it up
for your mother. Man, that talk was
just what the doctor ordered,
don't you think?"

I won't zing him for his enthusiasm today.

"It was awesome, Dad. I'll print it out
when I get home."

The bearded guy catches up with us
and puts a hand on Dad's shoulder.

"I'm Gary, and I'm pleased to meet you both."
He asks Dad to go for coffee
and I welcome the idea to find a chair
in the lobby to text Mia.
She would just be getting out of third period.

U can b proud of me, writer lady. Just took
tons of notes. Have to admit there's a
rush with it. That how u feel?

While waiting for an answer
I stroll towards the room I saw earlier
with all the people milling around.
The girl I saw in the meeting waves at me
across the lobby and walks toward me.

I remember her name from the introductions,
but she beats me to it.

"Hi, Claire, how did you like that meeting?"

"Hi. Yeah, I uh, really thought
there was some great stuff mentioned.
How about you?"

"Me, too. We found out about Brenda
and Jackson three years ago, but it
took my parents a while to get here. I think
we might be ahead of you."

"Ahead?"

"I mean, it sounds like you and your family
got the diagnosis pretty recently. Right?"

"Oh yeah, right." I point to the room
I'm curious about. "What's the attraction
in there?"

She pauses, and her eyes turn sad.
"It's the memorial wall.
You know,

the ones who have died
from Batten."

I put my hand to my mouth
maybe to stifle a scream
or the tears
already stinging my eyes.

"It's okay, Claire.
It was heavy for me, too,
the first time I saw it.
It helps
to know about it
before the names
appear.
It helps
to know about it
ahead of time."

GOLD MINE

Dad doesn't say anything
as he approaches
but his tight embrace
tells me he knows what
I've just discovered.
I don't try to stop the tears
as I cling to him.

"It's okay, baby. It's okay."

I'm aware Wendy is just standing there,
not gawking
but quietly waiting
for the storm to pass.

I pull away from Dad
and laugh through the last
sputtering tears.

"Thanks, Wendy. Thanks for
filling me in."

"No worries, Claire. See you
tomorrow."

Dad and I head to our room
and I notice Mia's text
that came in earlier.

> Yes! Proud of u.
> Nothing like getting to bottom
> of good story and u r sitting
> on pure gold. Cya

Hmmm. Sure depends
on how you define
pure gold.

SORRY FOR MYSELF

Wendy seeks me out at breakfast
and I welcome her suggestion
to sit together at the Sib meeting.

She doesn't seem to know any more
about it than I do.
I'm secretly glad
she lets on how she is a little nervous
like me. My nerves ratchet up a notch
when I see the room full of chairs
pulled up to round tables

centered with baskets full of
art supplies and big sheets of paper.
That always means group work,
something that doesn't come easily
for me.

We both relax about two minutes
into the meeting when the presenter
keeps popping one-liners
and never stops smiling.
She must be related to Gary,
the bearded guy.

I try not to look too nerdy
whipping out my notebook.
"Teacher requirement,
missing so much school."
I lie. Truth is,
feels like a security blanket.
        Note to self, check with Mia.
        Maybe that's the whole point.

The joking leader lady
manages to keep smiling
while jumping into some
serious stuff:
"Show of hands," she says.
        "Sorrier for yourself
                than the sibling(s)?
        Depressed?
        Guilty for being healthy?
        Need to be the good child?
        Angry at (fill in the blank)?
        Feeling left out?
        Need to achieve double (or triple)?
        Urge to talk to someone who understands?

Now go around the table.
Fess up to at least one of these gems,
then grab a piece of paper,
put yourself on the spot
and draw your hearts out.
You have twenty minutes."

Eyeballs roll, obviously reassessing
the joking lady's casual demeanor.
She means business,
            but somehow
                        it feels good.

It's a no-brainer for me
            and maybe for the others.
No one takes long
to choose,
and papers start filling up
immediately.

It takes a few intense minutes
before anyone feels like talking,
then self-deprecating comments
about the art work
start rolling around the table.
I realize I'm not the only one
actually getting into this.

I mostly listen and stare at my picture
with a silent chuckle.
For not being an artist
I think I got the point across.
            I'm sitting at the piano
looking
very,
very,
sorry
for myself.

PERMISSION

Before we break for lunch
we take turns sharing.
Some are clearly gifted artists
who have captured depths of emotion—
      gut-wrenching,
      soul-searing,
      pain-ridden
    facial expressions
accompanied by hilarious poses.
I'm struck by the contrast:
    deep,
        funny,
    deep,
        funny,
and a wave of remorse rolls over me
as I remember my words to Dad.

*...I just don't think it's a good idea
to be all happy...*

I walk out of the room
unable to talk
while my mind,
      my whole being
processes the message.

I've just been given permission
to laugh,
to cry,

and

to fully live this life,
my life
that has been spared.

TRAFFIC JAM

The lobby looks like a traffic jam
just like it did that first day.
     Wheelchairs and strollers
     parked every which way.
     Loud conversations,
     bursts of laughter,
     blank stares,

but in just four days,
     rather than threatening to strangle me,
the congestion in this room
feels like a family party
that I must leave too soon.

I say good-bye to Melissa,
     reach for her hand,
     squeeze it firmly,

hug her mom, Sharon,
squat down to talk to Brenda and Jackson,

exchange email and phone numbers
with Wendy,

and then I scan the room
looking for Dad.

I find him in the Memorial Room
standing a few feet away from the Wall,
studying it like a fine painting.

I slip my arm into his.
He hugs me close
and we let the tears

147

gently speak what neither of us
can say.

THE ROCK

I sink into the window seat,
glad for the two-hour flight home
to process this other planet
we've just visited
where dying children live and laugh and play
in all stages of dying,
and people who care for dying children
live and laugh and cry and talk and do and be

and...

"It was something, wasn't it babe?"

Dad reaches for my hand,
the one holding the rock.

"Tell me about this," he says, smiling big.

I return the big smile.
"It was so awesome, Dad. At first
Wendy and I thought it was cornball
like kid stuff
but afterward, we agreed it was way cool.
Sharon was our leader
you know, Melissa's mom,
and she had these river rocks
surrounding a jar of feathers.
We all got to pick one of each.
Maybe you can guess what they stand for."

"Clueless," Dad says, surrendering with hands up.

"Feather is for traveling light,
like shedding baggage—
        the stuff, well,
like the stuff I've been carrying around,
        maybe you, too,
dumb stuff like guilt, anger, resentment.

The rock is for dwelling deep.
This one's not so easy...
figuring out what or who you are
deep down in your core, you know
        solid,
        peaceful,
        rounded
like a river rock
and how you are going to
live it out,
        especially
given your life circumstances
at the moment.

Dad nudges my hand.
"Do I get to see what your deep
side is?"

"Only if you don't laugh
and if you recognize that I...
well, that I am a work in progress.
Sharon's words, not mine."

"Of course. I promise."

I slowly open my hand to reveal the drawing of
        a stick figure holding a bunch of balloons
        and under it
        the word

CELEBRATE.

Dad leans back in his seat and closes his eyes.
"I'm proud to call you my daughter, Claire.
Let's rest. We have lots of celebrating to do
when we get home."

HOW IT FEELS

My cell starts going bonkers
as soon as the plane taxis
towards the terminal.

Mia: Whoot! Whoot! So proud of you!

Tara: OMG go girl! BTW I knew u could do it.

Juan: Calls for a celebration!

I chuckle that my choice
of an intense four-day weekend
in Cincinnati has earned points
with my friends.

I remember the group therapy day
at Schmoozies and figure
this must be an extension of that
awesome "we're hear for you" moment.

Another ping:

Carlos: You rock, Claire!

And another:

Kyle: Claire in the winner's circle! Yay!

Winner's circle...
Winner's circle?

I nod absently as Dad waves from
the luggage carousel
and I dial Mia. My watch tells me
she should be just about sitting down
to homework.

"I'm dying to hear all about
Cincinnati, but first
how does it feel?"

"Well, I'm totally exhausted but
it's like I just pulled an all-nighter
to cram for a test
and now I'm ready to nail it,
know what I mean? Mia,
it was so awesome and..."

"I'm sure it was awesome, but wait,
you don't know, do you?
I can't believe they didn't call you
or text you or something..."

"What are you talking about?
I'm the exhausted one
but you aren't making any sense."

"You won the contest, you geeky girl.
You and your "Kite" won first place
            in the whole state of North Carolina.
Now how do you feel?"

                Numb...Davy...Too tired to feel
                anything...Trent...Not like I thought
                I would feel...Juan...Travel light...

too much baggage...celebrate?...
guilt...bad timing...way too tired...

"Hello, Earth to Claire, are you still there?
Did you hear me? YOU WON! Aren't you blown away
or what?"

I see Dad signal for me to head his way.
He has our bags.

"Yeah. Blown away is right on, Mia. Listen,
I *am* excited, I mean, really, but, uh
brain dead, you know?
Frankly, taken by surprise.
We'll catch up
tomorrow."

I hear hurt, misunderstanding in her voice
as she hangs up.
I follow Dad to the shuttle bus.

Geeky girl, there is something
seriously
wrong
with you.

IN THE WINNER'S CORNER

Dad points the car to our house,
a twenty minute drive from the airport.

"Why so quiet?"

pause

"Exhausted, I guess."

pause

"I know *I* am, but I can't wait to tell
your mother about all the good stuff
we've just experienced."

I weigh the words I want to speak.

Good stuff.

Good stuff?

Maybe I don't know what is
or is not
good stuff anymore.

Why does winning the contest feel
      so weird,
      so heavy,
      so opposite good stuff
      right now?

I feel Dad puzzling over my silence
while I long for time and space
to sort out the swirling confusion
that has invaded my head,
my heart.

"I won," I say in a small, flat voice,
      like the girl in Geometry
      who speaks so softly
      the exasperated teacher
      has to ask her to repeat it
      and half the time
      it's the wrong answer.
I look across the front seat

as the passing car headlights cast shadows
across my dad's face.

The car swerves slightly
as Dad jerks his head my way.
"You what?...You won?...The contest?
Why didn't you tell me?
When did you hear?"

My mouth won't move.

"This doesn't sound like the reaction
        of a winner, Claire.
        What's going on?"

I burst into tears.
        I'm not
        and
        I don't know.

AN ISSUE TO BE DEALT WITH

Dad pulls off the highway
        going too fast,
comes to an abrupt stop
at a convenience store parking lot
and kills the motor.

I search for a tissue in my pockets
and try to stop blubbering.
He stretches his arm across the gears
and pulls me as close as he can
for an awkward side hug
and then releases me
while I blow my nose.
He waits silently.

I can feel his impatience
and an inward sigh.
      Anger?
      Disgust?
      Disappointment?
      Disbelief?

Our faces take on a greenish glow
under the streetlight.
I think I might throw up.

I know my tired, efficient father
doesn't want to be dealing with
      an issue,
      my issue,
in a cold, dark car
a few blocks from home
after a long, emotional journey.

Neither do I.

...be the good child?...achieve double,
triple?...talk to someone?...feel guilty?

I try to push swirling, jumbled thoughts
out of my head
and focus on a steady voice.
"I can't explain it, Dad. Not now.
You know about overload. That's where
I am right now. Overload.
Can we sort of keep the contest news to ourselves,
not mention it to Mom and the boys,
until I can...
      until I can sort things out
      in my own head? Maybe a day
      or two?"

The look I get is perplexed.
The answer I get
after another long silence
is relieved.

"Sure, Claire.
Totally understandable.
Let's go home."

He let's out a long breath
and starts the engine.

WITHOUT A MUSICAL ACCOMPANIMENT

I just have time to take in
a few deep breaths,
       thinking how good
       a hot shower and my own bed will feel,
before we round the corner
and see the flashing lights at the
end of the block
       in front of our house.

Dad bumps up against the curb
and practically slams into the
fire engine.
We both jump out and race
for the front door, wide open
with two firemen standing on
the porch.

A medic comes out and spots Dad.
"You must be Mr. Fairchild?"

"Yes, of course, what's going on?
Where's my wife, the kids? Is it fire?

Someone hurt?"

The medic reaches for Dad's arm.
"Your wife is upstairs. I'm afraid
you've had a double header here tonight.
The oldest boy had a seizure
and apparently fell toward his brother,
knocking a tooth out. A few stitches
on his upper lip, and we're confident
your oldest son is stable.
Your wife is okay now.
She was a little beside herself
when we got here."

He pauses to give Dad a minute to absorb
it all, then he leans down to close his bag
and softens his voice.

"Your wife told me what you are up against, Sir.
Tough break. Don't hesitate to call us.
Good night now."

They leave,
probably as quickly as they had arrived.
Mom falls into Dad's arms, sobbing,
just inside the door.
They grab me
and we repeat the crying circle
that we had that first night.

We move as one into the family room
where Mom goes first,
filling in the details of a nightmare evening
that happened so fast
like a perfect storm,
she said,
just minutes after Dad's call

from the baggage claim
saying we were on our way home.

"Jan, we'll never do this again," he says.
We'll go as a family, like we should have
in the first place."

We talk into the night,
mostly Dad unloading his notes
and brochures
and positive outlook,
telling Mom
        not about a cure
but about hopeful things:
        research,
        networking with other families,
        Make-a-Wish Foundation,
        fund-raising.

I don't say much
but it occurs to me
before I say goodnight and head for bed
that Dad's voice sounds strong
and Mom's face looks peaceful
and the evening went,
        in spite of the perfect storm,
exactly as it should have gone

without a musical accompaniment.

FRAGMENTS

Davy and Trent show no signs
of their nightmare night, hugging
and hanging all over me at breakfast
and pestering me.

"Where did you and Dad go?
Why didn't we get to come, too?"

I catch pained looks on both parents' faces
as I ply them with questioning eyes.

we need to talk

Mom turns an exhausted face and forced smile
away from the lunches she's making.
"My calendar says we should be hearing
about the contest soon, Claire. Maybe today, huh?"

we need to talk

I hear Carlos honk out front.
I say hasty "good-byes,"
relieved to escape the frying pan
but dreading the leap into the fire.

It's "Tara Tuesday"
but she drops her usual banter
to shine the spotlight on me, leading
a bad rendition of
"For she's a jolly good fellow"
as I jump into the back seat.

Juan, his smile so genuine,
his words so real,
"No one deserves it more
than you, Claire."

we need to talk

Mia meets us near the lockers
"Well, Miss Snippet,

do I dare congratulate you
or give you my condolences?"
She's smiling but...

we need to talk

TALKING SOON

Wendy, my new friend,
texts me right before shutting down
my phone for first period.

Howzit going? Gr8 news. Brenda
accepted for clinical trial. Mtf.

A week ago I wouldn't have had a clue
about clinical trials. Now my heart skips a beat.

Plz tell me more. Cya.

Mia intercepts me in the hall on the way
to English, hands up like a cop halting traffic.
"Don't worry, I'm not bringing up the
contest. Just reminding you we have a date
with Mrs. Shepherd after school, um,
unless you're too busy."

"Mia, of course I want to come, and trust me,
I want to talk about the contest, but I need to
talk with Juan first."

The hint of romance perks her right up.
"Ah, of course you do, dearie. Why didn't I see
that? Seriously, he's okay with it, you know."

I do know, but I let her think it's his feelings

I have in mind.

> *And how does she know*
> *he's okay with it, anyway? Paranoia strikes again.*

I try unsuccessfully all day
to catch Juan alone.
While he gives me wide berth
I try sending mental messages:

> *...we need to talk soon*
> *I promise,*
> *talk soon...*

THE WORDS I NEED

Mia is occupied in the car
adjusting her recorder
while I occupy my brain
with various Juan thoughts.

What I want to say.
What I need to say.
What I can't say.
What I should say.
What I will say.

What?

Somewhere around a month ago,
a brother or two ago,
a keyboard ago,
a kite ago,
a seizure ago,
a night ago,

somewhere in there
are the words
I need for Juan.

THE CAUSE

I swear, Mrs. Shepherd looks more
and more like a little girl every time
we visit. Today it's pink bobby socks,
navy blue polyester slacks,
and a light blue cardigan over a
round-collared white blouse
and of course, the Day-Glo tennies.

Her eyes glisten like sparklers.
She ushers us to a back bedroom
where several chairs are arranged
around an old record player.

She motions for us to sit.
Her hands caress the worn cover
of the record on her lap as
her faraway voice transports us all into the past.
"Pete Seeger, Newport Folk Festival,1963.
Surprised the kids.
Didn't tell 'em 'til before dawn
when I hauled 'em out of bed,
even let 'em miss a couple days of school.
　　　Honey, here. You put this on for us.
　　　These ol' hands are too trembly."

She motions to me, I guess
because I'm closest to the player.
I suddenly feel trapped.

　　　Are we in for the whole record,
　　　the whole afternoon?

I glance at Mia, but she's whacking away
on her computer.
  "This Land is Your Land"
fills the room, soon followed by
   "Where Have All the Flowers Gone"

   and then

some sea chanteys neither of us knows.

Mia and I are both into it,
not ready to quit
when Mrs. Shepherd breaks the spell
and eases out of her chair
to take a chance on lifting the needle arm
herself.

"I reckon you girls don't want to stay
for the whole concert. As I recollect,"
her voice breathy as she falls back into her chair,
"we got onto this subject because of
hootenannies now, didn't we?"

We both smile and nod.

"Well, to finish the story...
Billy and Mary,
they wanted to know all about
Pete Seeger all the way home
and, well,
I told them everything I knew
second hand from Finley,
God rest his soul.

He was the one who brought
the music—more than that—

       the energy behind all those causes
       Seeger had,
into our house,
into our lives."

She closes her eyes.
Mia and I exchange glances
thinking once again, she's breathing her last.

Her eyes open wide and she pierces us
one at a time
with deep, probing gazes.
"Finley always had a cause, you see.
Got the idea from this man, Seeger.
He always had a cause
and Billy and Mary,
well, they caught on to it
and seems like we had causes
coming in and out of this little old house
until, well,
until God himself
brought it all to rest.
Yes, He did.
Those were some good years,
yes sir,
some mighty fine, good years."

Mia finds my eyes now,
and we both know it's time to go.

I want to hear the details about the causes
and how the hootenannies figured in
and how much money they raised,
       if that's even where Mrs. Shepherd is going,
and how long they had before,
       before God brought it all to rest.

My mind swirls
while Mia yammers on in the car about
her own excitement:
>"Do you realize what a super-awesome
>story this is going to turn into
>for the school paper,
>maybe even the city paper,
>like shades of the *NY Times*
>and Pulitzer material...?"

Mia's words fade
while something inside me quickens
like a piano string
being tuned.

REHEARSING

It's after five,
my usual time to watch the boys
and then I remember, Mom stayed home
with them today.
Maybe I should be there, too,
just in case,
after yesterday.
But instead, I text Juan.

>Schmoozies possible in 15?
>Know it's late, but REALLY need to talk.

I ask Mia's mom if she can drop me off
at Schmoozies, figuring I'll take my chances
on both Juan and Mom's reactions.
If not, I need think time.

>Mom, I need to stay for catch-up work.
>Be home by 6. Sorry.

Claire, Carlos can drop me in ten. J.

Claire, ok, but no later. Mom.

I slide into our back booth
and realize I am no closer
to knowing what it is I want to say
to Juan. I stare at my hands
splayed on the table in front of me.

You won the contest, you geeky girl.
  You won
    geeky girl.
      The contest.
       You won.

So what's the big deal, anyway?

BAD IDEA

Juan and his gorgeous smile
slide into the booth.
I blush
then blush even deeper
when he just locks into a stare
that won't quit.

"What?" I say, taking a deep slurp
of my smoothie.

"You know I'm proud of you, don't you?
I mean, sincerely glad you won;
  no personal garbage,
  no bad vibes,
just really happy for you.

You do know that, right?
I mean
it would bum me out
if I thought this came between us.
Man,
I've thought
about this
over and over
and..."

Now I return his lock-on stare.
"Juan, I *do* know
and I *am* relieved, too.
I spent as many hours as you did
wondering,
just wondering how it would feel
        one way or the other.

But..."

"Oh no. Now the reservations, right?"

"No. Yes. JUST LISTEN!"
I lower my voice when heads turn
on either side of us.

I hold my steady gaze
speaking slowly, softly, clearly.

"I can't explain it.
All I know is
things have changed.
I've changed.
I thought winning the contest
would be so awesome
and when you all texted me

about winning, I didn't feel excited
or thrilled
or anything good. I felt
nothing but
bad."

Juan leans his puzzled face toward me.

"Bad? What do you mean, bad?
I'm not sure I'm tracking."

"Bad like a bad dream, maybe.
It's been coming on for a while, Juan.
I'm not sure I can explain it.
It's like competing to be the best musician,
         competing to be the best at anything
seems so pointless now.
But especially the music...
what's it all worth in the end?
It's so selfish, all those hours
practicing, polishing, rehearsing,
It isn't going to make a difference
in anybody's life."

"I get it. Your brothers are really weighing
on you, aren't they?"

I fight to hold back the tears
and anger.

"Of course, Juan. How would they not?"

"I understand, Claire. I know that part
of your life has changed, but music's
been your whole life,
your dream
forever.

How can you just dump it
when you're at the top
of your game?

"That's just it. Maybe it's not *my game.*
Maybe it was the game my parents
picked out for me.
I don't feel the music in me at all.
It feels dead.
My fingers feel dead,
like they are pounding pieces of ivory
that I can't hear or feel.
I want to walk away from it all. I'm sorry
I ever entered the contest, and if I could
ditch the recital, the summer program,
the scholarship, all of it, I would."

A look I can't read passes over Juan's face
as he pulls away from me,
sinking with a thud
against the back of the booth.

"Wow, Claire. You sound really

    depressed.

That's it. You *are* depressed.

But you just can't,
I mean,
you can't just bail.
You won, and well,
now you have to deal with it."

"I'm *not* depressed, Juan.
Deal with it? What's that supposed to mean?
Deal...with...it?

169

I need to go."

"Deal with being a winner, Claire.
You're the winner."

I slide out of the booth,
awkward,
too hot
and dry-eyed.

GUILTY DAY

I'm twenty minutes
and a flood of tears late
and Mom lights into me.
        Understandable,
but the circles under her eyes,
the household clutter, the marked
acting-out in a once-mellow Trent—
all feed the hurricane going on
inside my head.

"Come on, guys, this room's a disaster.
Help me clean it up

now."

I remember what they said at BDSRA
about keeping things "normal,"
having reasonable expectations
about everyday things
        as long as possible,
        that is.
What they didn't mention
was how the healthy members
of the family are supposed

to keep things normal.

Trent grumbles.
"Don't give me any lip," I say, mock-seriously.
"Get it? Lip? Yucca, yucca, yucca."

I ruffle his hair then wonder
if I just went too far,
            like I did with Juan today,
but Trent laughs and I quickly ask,
"How is it today, buddy? Sore, I'll bet."

He tugs at the part of his lip
that isn't in stitches for my inspection.

"Eew, gross," I say dramatically
and Davy chimes in, too,
even though I know he can't see it
that well.

Mom goes to bed soon after the boys.
I almost make it to my room
when Dad looks up from his papers.

"Things any better today, Claire?"

Better? How could they be any worse?

"I'm working on it, Dad. Maybe tomorrow?"
He nods, and I escape to my room,
not sure at all
how many tomorrows
it would take to make sense
out of life
right now.

Winter Part 2

be-CAUSE

The clock says I'd better get
to homework sometime soon
      but I see Mia is still on FB
      so I message her.

Desperate to unload.

      Start from the beginning. Homework done.

My fingers fly. I start with BDSRA,
the intense emotions that saturated me
and Dad from the first lobby experience,
      jammed with wheelchairs and strollers
      and smiling, drooling children in all stages
      of the disease;

to informational lectures on
      genetics,
      clinical trials,
      family dynamics,
      treatment plans;

to teen support groups,
      meeting Wendy,
      the corny art projects,
      sharing feelings I didn't know I had.

Awesome, but I thought this was
to be about Juan.

      Ikr. Juan.
      Man, I blew it today.
      What I wanted to say to him
      came out all wrong
      or he took it the wrong way

and he just thinks I'm depressed
and...

Well spit it out Gf.
Don't stop typing if you
insist on crying.

Su, My-yah, Me-yah. I think
I cried it out on the walk home.

I tell her how winning the contest
just doesn't seem
important
anymore.

I tell her how I felt
when I stood in front of the memorial wall
and realized all those sick kids,
including Davy and Trent,
would never get the thrill of entering
or winning
any kind of contest
and the greatest contest they have going
is to win
another
day's breath.

Then at Mrs. Shepherd's...
Pete Seeger and his causes;
it's like I've been handed a cause
and now I need to know what to do with it.

But I still don't get how Juan figures...

It's getting late, and there's homework,
but I need Mia to get it.

Don't want to spend another second
celebrating me.
Don't want to be like Mrs. Shepherd.
Regret not celebrating brothers' lives.
Want to start now. Ditch recital,
scholarship, summer camp.
I'm sure Juan came in second.
Working up to telling him
I want to forfeit…

Plz tell me you didn't do that…

NW. He got weird.
Accused me of being depressed.
Ranted about how I'm the winner
and I just need to DEAL WITH IT.
I left.

Dad sees my light.
Getting the bedtime harass.
Talk tomorrow.

NIGHT RIDE

wheelchairs flying through the lobby
and I can't get out of mine they have
me strapped in and the line is long and
very hot and my name isn't on the list
yet but someone said it should be but
Davy can't get the wheelchair off the
ceiling and I'm afraid I will fall out
so Trent rescues us just in time for the
demonstration where they show us how
to make the wheelchair do the walking
for us when it is time to go up the hill
where the banner full of names of those

who have been accepted into the secret
club is blowing in the wind like a multi-
colored kite and suddenly the string
breaks and the kite flies away while I
watch Davy and Trent float up to find it.

LOST CAUSE

I corner Mom and Dad,
both in the kitchen at the same time
for breakfast.

"Any chance we can have a talk
tonight, after the boys are in bed?"

Dad winks and gives me a knowing nod
while Mom looks concerned.

"Nothing's wrong.
I just need...want to talk to you both.
It's all good, Mom, really," I say,
flashing a smile full of confidence
I do not feel.
They agree.

Carlos honks.

Whew. Got the easy one out of the way.
But where do I begin with Juan?
Obviously not in the car
in front of Carlos.

First no one says anything
then Carlos mumbles a hesitant
"Hey, Claire"
as if he's been forewarned

and then, barely audible,
without turning around
Juan utters a limp "Hey."

Tara, why aren't you here
when I need you?

Dead silence all the way to school.
I practically jump out
before Carlos stops,
hoping to get far enough ahead
in case the tears won't wait
until the nearest bathroom.

HE'S A GUY

Mia grabs me two minutes before
first period bell.

"You look gruesome, dearie.
Before you tell me how you
didn't sleep, want my take on Juan,
'cause I DID sleep on it?"

"Do I have a choice?"

Mia doesn't skip a beat.
"It all figures. The look he gave you.
The snarky response.
He's a guy, for God's sake.
A tremendously talented,
gorgeous hunk
with a big ego, and when he
heard you dissing the big win,
        in spite of his noble intentions,
        he let his all-too-human feelings out

and he had a jealous hissy fit, that's all.
He had a big moment of
'It should have been me after all.'
How could he not?
Listen, Dumbo. How could you
expect him to take it
any other way?"

I let her words sink in.

"So,
um,
any suggestions?"

"That's simple. Just keep your prize.
Go through the motions
and then do what you need to do
to celebrate your brothers, as you say."

"No way."

"Why?"

"be-CAUSE."

THE CONTEST CONTINUES

I slam the door on the nearest stall
and let loose with the tears.

> How can I fix the mess with Juan
> if he won't speak to me?

> Maybe Mia's right about going ahead
> with the whole thing.

What good is a good cause for my brothers
if everything else is messed-up?

Someone rushes in from the hall
finishing a conversation and popping gum.
I know immediately
who it is.

I flush the toilet, blow my nose,
brace myself, and make like I'm
in a rush.

"Claire! I was just sayin' to Carlos
how awesome it is that you won,

      pop, pop

and I know how you and Juan
worked so hard and all,

      snap, pop

...girlfriend, you've been cryin'
haven't you? And Juan looks
like death warmed over.
Like we were all worried this would
come between you two and now look,
it's got you both upset.
Anything I can do to help?"

      pop, snap

"No thanks. I'm afraid the contest
isn't over yet."

I head for the door.
Tara stops applying more lipstick

in mid-air and stares with her mouth open.

"What? But I thought..."

"Later, Tara. I'll explain later."

THE DISCONNECT

I have a few minutes
before the boys get home.
I sit down at the piano.
I find the opening notes of "The Kite,"
        first time since the conference.
I search for the old connection—
        the moment of release
        between a soaring mental image
        and my fingers,
        and the smooth rippling of ivory keys
        dancing at my command;

but

        all I see in my mind is a swirling spiral of color
        shooting off into a high wind
        and the release of pressure
        as the line snaps.

I stop playing.
This is what I was trying to explain to Juan.
The line between me and music
has snapped.

I look down.
I used to talk to these hands.
        How can life change
        so drastically
        in just a few months?

MAKING WISHES

The doorbell rings.
Davy and Trent's carpool moms
have taken to escorting them to the door
since both boys have tripped on the stairs
more than once.

I thank the driver and
give extra big bear hugs
to my brothers.
It feels good to be back
on after-school duty as I
guide my brothers
into the kitchen for a snack.

"I wish I could have gone
on a trip with Dad all alone,"
Davy says with his mouth full
of popcorn.

"Yeah? Well maybe you can sometime.
Where would you go if you could
go anywhere you wanted?"

Davy works on another mouthful
of popcorn but doesn't take long
to answer.

"I'd go someplace with a gazillion
video games to choose from
and play all day and never stop
playing even for bedtime."

He makes some familiar Nintendo sounds,
mimics using the control buttons,
and then breaks out laughing.

"I'd like to see that myself. What
about you, Trent?"

He has an instant answer.
"I'd like to see a Dallas Cowboys game
and meet Tony Romo. That would be so cool."

He makes a few quarterback moves
and "pshew" sounds of a whizzing ball.

"Why am I not surprised at that one?"

Mental note: Add Make-a-Wish
Foundation to our conversation tonight.

PAINFUL EXPLANATION

Mom looks so exhausted
I think maybe we should skip
our talk. I wonder how long it will be
before she considers part-time teaching
or taking a leave of absence.

I take a cue from Dad,
who pours another cup of coffee
for both of them
and leads us all to the den.

Suddenly I'm nervous
on the spot,
feeling their stares boring into me
expectantly, so I let it just roll out.

"Mom, I did win the contest, but..."

Shock and confusion flash across her face.
"What? Honey, that's fantastic! I *knew* you
would win all along."

Coffee splashes out of her cup as
she jumps up to hug me.
The light in her eyes,
the brightest I've seen in months,
quickly fades as she pulls back
from my tense body.

"But what, Claire? Is something wrong
about the contest, about winning?
You're not excited?"

Dad looks back and forth
between Mom and me,
compassion and sadness in his eyes.
He says it might make more sense
if we back up.
He asks me to fill Mom in
on the parts of BDSRA that meant the most
to me.

I do what he asks and then
the words come out easier.

"I can't do music anymore.
I don't *want* to do it anymore.
I wish I hadn't entered the contest.
Is there any way I can
forfeit the award to the
one, to whoever came in second?"

The bomb that just landed in
our living room threatens to blow up
in my face.

The silence is deafening,
the stunned looks are frozen.

BAD IDEA AGAIN

From the look on his face
my words didn't make any sense to Dad
or maybe
more sense than he can handle.
Mom sniffles and dabs at her eyes
for a long, awkward moment.

She blows her nose and takes
the schoolteacher role.
"Of course you feel bad, sweetie.
There's been so much with the boys
and their illness and it's totally
understandable that you would
feel overwhelmed
or a little depressed about things now,
but you don't really mean..."

Heat and a racing heart
threaten to choke my words.

"Mom, I mean every word.
I can't play anymore. It's like
I've lost it. Every time
I try, I think of Davy and Trent
and it all seems so useless,
so pointless to diddle away
at the keyboard while they
are dying. I can't focus.
I'm wasting my time.
I'm wasting my life

while their lives are
so, so, ruined.
My fingers don't even feel
the same. I need to be doing
something else, something
that could help them,
or help fight the stupid
dumb disease
somehow,
something
besides just making noise."

Dad, also the teacher,
chooses his words carefully.
"I see you have strong feelings
about what's happening
with your brothers,
and I appreciate your telling us.
While I may not agree with your
assessment of music in your life
at the moment,
you certainly have the right to be thinking
about alternative life goals for yourself;

     however,

right now
you have a commitment, an obligation
to carry through with the responsibilities
of the contest, that is
the recital,
the scholarship,
and the summer program."

I ask to be excused.
I retreat to my room
to try to make sense

out of the swirling mess
I've made out of my life.

NO CLUES

I slog through another day
of the silent treatment from Juan.
Thank God it's Tuesday
so Tara takes over the car
conversation and for now, Juan has taken
to going straight to class
and eating lunch at a different table.

Mia and I eat alone.
She suddenly stops eating and stares
wide-eyed just past my left ear.
I turn to follow her gaze
to the table across the cafeteria
where Juan and Tara are
eating lunch
side-by-side.

"So I never thought Juan
could be such an ass," Mia says.
I'm not sure if she's referring
to his choice of lunch partners
or his choice of words the other day.

Just deal with it.

And if I don't, does that make me another
barnyard animal—
          a chicken?

I'm not surprised at Mia's candor
but she winces when she hears

that Juan and my father
are on the same page.

"So don't get me wrong.
I'm not in their camp but I guess
I don't see what the big deal is
either. Why don't you just go
through with the recital
and the summer program,
take the scholarship and then
do whatever you need to do
for your brothers?"

I shake my head.
"Mia, the truth is,
I don't know if I *can* do it.
Something has really changed
deep down inside
since the conference.

Something has broken inside me.
I can't explain it.
Maybe it's guilt,
maybe it's fear.
Maybe it's just a huge
hurting hole that needs to be filled
up with living life for my brothers
instead of just for myself."

"Whoa! You're serious, right?"

"I am dead serious..."

My hand clamps over my mouth
at the horror of my choice of words.
Mia waits wide-eyed
while I recover.

"So what are you going to do?"

"You mean about the lunch situation
over there
or the contest?"

"Both."

"I
don't
have
a
clue."

SETTING AN EXAMPLE

Kyle gives me a ride home
realizing my ride has fallen through
at the moment. He's careful
not to take sides,
says he's sorry Juan and I
are "having issues."
I don't try to explain.

"So why don't you talk it out with him?"

I shake my head.
"Been there, done that
and really blew it, by the way."

"Aw come on, Claire. You guys
are too much of a fixture to stay
broken."

"Mia put you up to this?"

He drops me at my door
firmly denying it with
a Cheshire cat grin
and a hollered "maybe"
out the window.

I stand in the driveway and give it a try.

       Juan, can we talk?

The immediate response makes me wince.

       I have no problem with that.
       BTW, you were the
       one who ditched.

I have a strong urge to fling my phone
across the yard,
sling my backpack into the door
and scream obscenities
at the top of my lungs,

when the boys' carpool pulls in
and I suddenly remember
I'm the big sister,
       the one who sets good examples.

AVOIDANCE

I avoid Dad when he comes in the door.

I avoid him by retreating to my room
       like last night
              and like long ago,
on days when I knew

I wasn't ready for the piano lesson
the next day.
Even though he wasn't my teacher,
Mrs. Cobb was his friend,
and Dad would find out.
He never said anything
but I knew he got a report
and I knew
I had let him down.

Davy and Trent don't run from Dad.

It was a day without complications
full of the wonder two little boys can experience.

> One with limited vision,
> compromised physical abilities and
> diminishing mental capacities.

> One with the same venomous genes
> gathering momentum
> before striking their first blow.

They jockey for Dad's attention
and he pours it on thick
with exaggerated exuberance
over Davy's Mario brothers feat
and Trent's football maneuver
on the playground.

I sit on the side of my bed
savoring the sounds
of uncomplicated,
well-deserved
joy.

...right now

you have a commitment, an obligation
to carry through with the responsibilities.

Deal with it.

SITCOMS AND SHOULDS

The script at dinner could have been lifted
from a 1960's "Ozzie and Harriet" rerun:

> Hi, Mom.
> Hi, Pop.
> I had a swell time at school today.

Mom, Dad, and I have perfected
the new sitcom
we perform for the boys
almost daily.
Everyone,
everything
is peachy keen.

As soon as dinner cleanup is done
I head to my room
again,
close the door
and try to figure out how to patch it up
with Juan.

> *I've changed...*
> *Things have changed...*
> *I want to shift the focus...*
> *Music isn't the same...*

or maybe
just maybe

I should concentrate on hearing
what *he* has to say.

READY TO TALK, READY TO LISTEN

I pull out my homework
and try to concentrate on it
instead of Juan's last text,

> you were the
> one who ditched

that sits unanswered.

I start with the nonfiction
writing assignment, trying to decide
between a profile of Mrs. Shepherd
or a fact piece on Batten disease.
Making a decision with such scattered thoughts
may not be the best idea.
Batten wins.

After all, knowledge is power, isn't it?

My focus quickly evaporates...

Maybe it would be better
if he told me he doesn't want to talk
ever again.
Then we could both move on,
get over it.

Maybe he's already over it.

Maybe we weren't the good old friends
I thought we were all along.

Maybe my suspicions about him and Mia
  aren't just paranoia after all.

Maybe this is just how it will end
in a cloud of misunderstanding.

I grab my phone and give in to
pride,
total distraction,
loneliness,
desire.

   Ygtr. I was the ditcher.
   Can we try it one more time
   at Schmoozies after school tomorrow?

Quick response.

   I'm game. Cya there.

DEAL WITH IT

I beat Juan to Schmoozies
and let my imagination rip:
he'll slide into the same side of the booth,
tighten his arm around my shoulder,
spread the warmth of his body
next to mine and
reassure me that we are still
who we've always been—
   good friends—
and not two alien beings
inhabiting the same familiar bodies.

   but you   *have changed*
 things *are different*

things   are not   the same
          as they used to be

I force a smile when he comes through the door,
casual but cool,
and slides in across from me.

"Hey."

I take in as much air as I can to avoid sounding
tentative, or nervous, or God-forbid
          condescending.

"Thanks for coming, Juan."

His smiling eyes encourage me
to breathe easier
and I remember my vow
to listen to what he has to say.

"So, I'm sorry
about the other day" I say.

"Yeah, me too."

Silence.

"You go first."

Silence.

"Look, whatever you do about
the contest...that's your call,
and not something I care to think about,
but I do still care about music,
a lot,
like it will probably be my life—

useless and pointless,
no, selfish
as it is."

Juan stares me down,
strangling me with the straw paper
he slowly wraps around his finger
and the echo of words that came out of
my
own
mouth.

"I never meant..."

"It's okay, Claire.
I get it now.
And I *did* mean what *I* said
the other day."

Now he takes his turn
and silently ditches
on me.

You're the winner.
Deal with it.

MUSIC OR ME?

I'm too stricken to cry.
Juan's words echo in my head
like a menacing alarm,
like an alarm I need to pay attention to.

You're the winner.
Deal with it.

Winner?
How can there be a winner
in this game?
How can I pretend to be a winner
in the middle
of so much
loss?

Deal with it?
How do you deal with being a winner
in a no-win situation?

Useless.
       Pointless
              Selfish.

Music or me?

DEALING WITH DREAMS AND REALITY

Juan is on a huge stage,
a single spotlight zooms in on his fingers
fluttering like hummingbirds
on glistening flute keys.
I listen to his music
from somewhere backstage,
interrupted by the noise
of a hammer and saw.
Someone is building something.
It looks like a new house
for Davy and Trent
and there is a girl standing nearby
watching, maybe even supervising
the work in progress.
It's a peaceful dream,
a sense that everything is working

according to the plan.
The peace follows me
when I wake up
and I know I am ready
to deal with it

somehow.

I know I have less than a month
           to get "The Kite" in shape
           for the recital.

I know that the scholarship will
           "help with expenses."

I know the summer camp will
           "broaden my horizons."

I know that trying to talk with Juan,
           at least right now, is futile.

I know I'll find a way to help my brothers.

I know that wasting my time feeling sorry for myself
           needs to be a feather
           not a rock.

I know that celebrating life needs to be a rock
           not a feather.

I know it might not be a bad day after all
           if I keep this up.

ORBITING BODIES

Juan and I end up at the lockers
           at the same time

on this last day
before Christmas break,
and we both slam the doors
maybe a bit too hard
      at the same time,
resulting in a mutual laugh,
the first one since what feels like
forever.

We're back to talking
      but like everything else in my life
it's not the same as it once was.
We don't talk about the contest
or anything beyond the surface,
and our bodies
seem to be orbiting around the same sun
but safely locked into wide-apart paths
with no chance of ever
falling into sync
      or colliding.

But I've promised myself to be thankful for
      what is
without bemoaning
      what is not.
We head for Carlos's car
as I hammer Juan with questions,
      genuine questions
      about his family's upcoming Colorado ski trip
      since I've never been there.

When I start to get out of the back seat
he turns around
and flashes the smile
that still melts me inside
and the eyes
that still seem to search

to the bottom of my soul.

I'm glad I have the vacation away from him.
Maybe I can discover what's shifted
in our galaxy.

GOLDILOCKS

I use the time before the boys show up
to run through "The Kite,"
and this time,
something new and different—
like Goldilocks,

> not too hot,
> not too cold,
> but just right.

I surprise myself and let loose.
> *Is this how Juan does it?*

Arpeggios fly
> not too big,
> not too small,
> but just right,

into an improvisation that lands
> on the keyboard

> not too hard,
> not too soft,
> but just right.

I work myself and my "piece"
into a frenzied crescendo.
I'm astounded,

like Goldilocks,
that I hung in threatening territory
(the keyboard)
and survived
without being eaten alive
by the bears
in my thoughts.

I wonder:
did Goldilocks have courage
to venture
into the forest again?

WE LOVE YOU, MRS SHEPHERD

I remember how I tagged along
with Mia on her first interview with
Mrs. Shepherd, sort of ho-hum,
feeling like a third wheel,
and now I can't wait to see her again.

"That lady grows on you, doesn't she?"

"Isn't she just the most darling person
you've ever met?" Mia asks while
clicking away on her iPad in the car.

"I'd like to meet this lady myself,"
Mia's mom says, "and I'd like to
be in such good shape at that age."

"Oh Mom, and you should have her
sense of style too, right, Claire?"

We both break into giggles.
Mrs. Shepherd doesn't let us down
this time, with fuchsia sweats

and a vintage, faded Pete Seeger T-shirt
that says
> "the right song
> at the right moment
> can change history."

I jot that down in my notes
and then Mia signals me
to pull out the Christmas present
we got her, an LP called
> "American Folk Songs for Children"
> by Pete Seeger.

Her eyes sparkle and tears seem to well-up
as she turns the record over
and around and around
in her gnarled, shaky hands.

"Now what'd you go and do this for, Missies?"

"We just wanted to, 'cuz we appreciate all the time
you've given us," Mia says.

We both say "we love you, Mrs. Shepherd."

She sets the record down next to her chair
and aims her glazed eyes at us.

"I suppose you want to hear
how they both went,
my Billy and Mary."

We nod, and I tighten the hold
on my pen.
> *Yes, I've been wanting*
> *and dreading*
> *to hear this.*

BILLY AND MARY

"He was comin' home late
from his first good job,
a reporter for the Hillsdale Tribune.
It's defunct now after all these years,
but he loved it. Wanted to be a writer
like you, Mia. Apart from music,
words were his thing
and he worked 'em around real good
so the news he reported grabbed you
right here."

She raises a shaky hand to her heart.

"It was right out there, just two miles
down that road. Drunk driver came
'round the corner and it didn't take
but a second. They both died instantly.
He was 27 years old...so many stories
he had yet to put into that paper,
so many
untold stories..."

Mia and I stay silent
watching for signs of exhaustion.
She sighs heavily and continues.

"Mary, my sweet, sweet little girl,
already had the sickness in her
when Billy left.
Doctors found the tumor in her brain
six months before
and she lived exactly six more months.
Died on her 25th birthday
and that after a terrible lot of sufferin'."

Mrs. Shepherd stays dry-eyed
but we both blow noses and wipe eyes,
trying not to make too much noise.
The fatigue finally catches up with her
and we know it's time to go.
Mia thanks her again
and musters all her cheeriness
to lift the mood.
In the car we both kick ourselves
for not having saved the present until last
   to end on a lighter note.
I do the math in my head.
I can't get over
how little time she had
with her children.

How
very
little
time.

GETTING THE BALL ROLLING

I can never sleep late
during vacations
and neither can Mom.
We both end up in the kitchen
early this first Saturday morning
while the house is still quiet.
I savor the time to catch up.
I want to tell Mom
about my Goldilocks moment
and my resolve to "deal with it."
I want to tell her Mrs. Shepherd's story
about Billy and Mary,
and how it makes me realize time

is ticking away in our family.
I want to tell her that I think
we need to do

SOMETHING...

but one look at the exhaustion
spread over her face
tells me it's not the right time.

Her thoughts are more immediate.

"I don't know what to do about
Christmas this year,
presents, I mean, for the boys..."

I see tears welling in her eyes.
Her heaviness threatens to weigh us
both down.

feathers and rocks

"Let me grab my computer, Mom.
I think this is a workable problem."
I dash to my room as quietly as possible,
experiencing an unexpected surge of
energy,
optimism,   hopefulness,
resolve.

I Google "toys and games for those with special needs."
Mom pours herself another cup of coffee
and pulls her chair next to mine.
I feel her body relax, as she sighs
and blows her nose.

"Voilà," I say, as I hit on a list

by category
of everything imaginable
for visually and physically handicapped
children.

"Oh, go back. Look,
look at that one, Claire."
Mom can't hide her excitement,
pointing to a soccer ball
with bells. "See if you can find
a football."

She scribbles on a notepad
and within five minutes
we have a list going:
      MP3 players.
      A talking interactive game called 'Bop It.'
      Tactile Tic Tac Toe.
      Wooden puzzles in all shapes and sizes.
      Talking watches.

Mom grabs my hand
and speaks deep into my eyes.

"Claire, do you think it's too early
for Trent? I mean, with no symptoms,
sometimes it's hard
to realize that, you know, that..."

The Memorial Room flashes in my brain
like a neon sign.

My brothers' laughter
when they play together rings in my ears.

The DNA test results fly before my face
like the handwriting on the wall.

"I think this is the right thing, Mom.
I think we are doing
just exactly
the right thing."

"Thanks, honey. I know you
are struggling, too, and I confess
I'm not always tuned in to your needs.
I've been thinking
you and Dad and I
should have more—
what should we call them—
therapy sessions?"

"I'm all for it, Mom. How about
tonight?"

I catch her off guard,
then she smiles big.

"Well then,
tonight it is."

MY NEW WORLD

Working on a Christmas gift list
for my two brothers with
visual and physical handicaps;

planning for a "therapy session"
with my parents;

hoping for a renewed friendship
with my oldest friend;

playing the piano without

worrying about competing;

dealing with a contest I would
rather avoid;

wondering how I can kick Batten
in the butt—

> is how you define
> my new world.

SNOW DAZE

Snow doesn't stick around long
in our climate,
so we wake the boys up
and all five of us
head for the backyard
dressed in makeshift winter gear.

Free from obstacles of movement,
Davy and Tent roll in it,
eat it,
throw it,
build with it,
run and laugh and shout in it,
and practically use it all up
before it can accumulate

and then
without any warning,

Dad rushes to Davy
who has fallen over
and is in the throes of another
grand mal seizure.

Mom grabs Trent and steers him inside
motioning me to help Dad with Davy.
We move him on his side.
Dad takes off his glove,
wipes saliva and mucous away from Davy's mouth
and as we have learned to do,
we let the seizure run its
short but interminable course.
When he comes around
we help him into the house,
out of his wet clothes
and onto his bed.
Mom has Trent in the kitchen
with a cup of hot chocolate
when I join them.

"Are seizures just part of growing
up, Mom, like growing pains? 'Cause
that would mean I'm probly going to get
them too, huh?"
Trent takes a big slurp
as if he had just asked
why the sky is blue.

Mom shoots a glance at Dad
and me
and for a frozen instant
we are all speechless.

Dad clears his throat.
"Not exactly, Trent.
Sounds like you have some
questions we need to talk about.
When Davy is feeling better
we'll all have that talk, okay buddy?"

It's time to tell them the truth.
They deserve to know
the
truth.

I lock Dad in a burning gaze
that might as well have been a battle cry
lost in the wind.

A DATE WITH GOOGLE

The house is quiet
the rest of the afternoon
and in spite of—
            maybe because of—
the morning crisis,
I wander around idly
on Google.

What am I looking for?

A soul salve.
A simple solution.
A cure
or at the very least,
something to make the
sadness less sad.

One stop tells me I could fill out the forms
in fifteen minutes,
form 1023
to become a 501 (c) (3).
That's what you call a charitable organization,
        or a foundation.

Way too big and besides
there are already big public charities
raising money.

Off the top of my head
I click in "how to raise money for a good cause"
and land on a site with corny pictures
that at least looks more user-friendly.
I scroll down:
>   Grant Applications.
>   Handling Funds.
>   Tax Limitations.
>   Setting up Bank Accounts.
>   Mission Statements.

Mrs. Shepherds' husband, Finley, always had a cause
but I'll bet it wasn't this complicated...

I'm about to click off
when I get to the last section,
Fundraising Ideas:
>   bake or craft sale,
>   host a party,
>   set up a booth at an event,
>   hold a raffle,
>   have a car wash,
>   put on a benefit concert.

It's as if the computer just called my name.
These things,
all of them,
are doable.

I want to tell someone—
Mia, and especially Juan.
It would make it more real
to share the excitement I feel

all the way down to my toes
but I resist the temptation
to grab my phone.

Instead, I open a Word document
and begin making notes.

CRYING OUT FOR ANSWERS

The uplift in my spirits
isn't reflected around the dinner table.
Davy's increased seizures have hit Mom hard,
along with the only real change in Trent,
his wakefulness at night.

She's simply sleep-deprived.
I heard just enough of her conversation with Dad
to know that the afternoon wasn't pleasant
after Davy woke up from his post-seizure nap.
I worry about the nose dive
she's taken
since the diagnoses.

I try to send Dad a mental message
that we could use a dose of his silly jokes
about now, but his sense of humor
seems to be on hold, too.

I think about bagging the plans
for our evening meeting
when my thoughts are interrupted
by the only dinner conversation so far.
Now it's Davy asking a question.

"Dad, did you have seizures when you
were my age?"

For a split second, Dad looks like
he's going to burst into tears.

It takes him a long time
for his one word answer. "No."

I want to shout my father down,
scream at him,
ask him if he can't see or hear
my brothers
crying out for answers.

I bite my tongue
and put this subject
at the top of our evening's agenda.

UNFAVORABLE CLIMATE

Mom looks apologetic
plopping onto the couch
after the boys are in bed,
announcing how exhausted she is.
Dad looks pained,
          maybe at both of us,
and musters a glimmer of his humor
as he looks directly at me
with "this meeting is called to order."

Mom perks up to give Dad a positive report
on our Christmas shopping decisions.
She gives me an "I love and appreciate you"
smile, and I take a deep breath before
plunging into what's hot on my brain,
          not what's spelled out in my notes
          from this afternoon.

"Dad, Mom, I know I can't tell you
how to raise my brothers, but
well, I just think they need—
        no, they deserve—
some answers to the questions
they are coming up with.
And it's not the first time
I've heard them. I just haven't
said anything."

Mom immediately starts crying
and Dad jumps up to pace.
It's now clear they are divided
on this issue, and it's not the first time
they've had this discussion.

Dad confirms my observations
and spells it out.
Mom wants to tell them at least something
about what they are facing
and Dad does not.
I can see both sides
and I can see I clearly don't have a vote
in this issue.

Worst of all
I can see that the climate is not favorable
for any kind of discussion
about my fundraising ideas,
        not now,
        maybe not ever.

I'm the one close to tears
as the meeting comes to an abrupt end.
I trudge upstairs
        dragging my rock of celebration
                by a string.

AFTERTHOUGHT

Oh, and BTW
Dad, Mom,
you'll be glad to know
I'm really dealing with the music
just like you wanted me to:
> *recital,*
> *summer camp,*
> *the scholarship;*
all forging ahead.
You remember...
That contest I entered
in a previous life?

LATE NIGHT MESSAGE

I need to talk to someone.

I start a text to Juan:
> delete.
I start a text to Mia:
> delete.
Like a really stupid rat
in an uncomplicated maze,
I go back and forth
with a string of attempts
to communicate with
the two people I know the best.

I hit a dead end every time.

I toss my phone on the bed
thinking about crawling in and putting
an end to this day that had such promise,

but just so I can get the urge to talk
out of my system
I email Wendy from BDSRA.

I ask her
how her family handled
the issue of telling her siblings
the truth, or at least some of the truth.
I realize as I click away
how good it feels to have this connection
with someone who really
understands what's going on in my life.
I wonder if I'll get to that point
with old friends
like Mia and Juan?

I jump as a message comes in.
My heart takes off in triple time
when I see it's not Wendy.

It's Juan.

APOLOGIES

Breathe. Breathe.

Hey.
So I hit a tree today
on the slopes…

Gasp.

OMG, are you OK?
In the hospital? What happened?

Nothing broken.

217

Just my pride lol.
I can't stop thinking about you, Claire.
The tree and the leaves, remember?
They go together. Kwim?
I miss you.
Miss talking with you.
Lots of time to think
on the slopes.
I've been an ass, and I'm sorry. Smh
When I uncurled myself from that tree
I thought about how stuff like pride
rules our lives sometimes,
kwim?

      I'm sorry too. I'm the one who screwed up.
      I didn't think about anyone's feelings but my own
      when it all happened so fast.
      Lots to tell you
      when you get back.
      Good stuff.

Awesome. Coming home early on Friday.
Bad luck to try Schmoozies
a third time?

      I'm game.
      Supposed to be a charm, right?

Yeah. Third time. Schmoozies. Cya at 4.

THE FEATHER NAMED PRIDE

If not for my clock that says 3:00 a.m.
I would be tempted
to fling open the window

and shout love with a capital 'J'
into the cold, starry night.

Third time's a charm.
Third time's a charm.

I settle for snuggling under my downy quilt
to think about Schmoozies on Friday
and feathers,
            especially one named pride
that was unleashed in my room tonight.
I picture it floating out my window
into the stratosphere,
gone, at least for now.

And across the room
on a shelf sits a rock
pulling me towards
a whole new interpretation
of the word *celebrate:*

life left to live
with Davy and Trent

and

friendship with Juan.

HOPING FOR THE BEST

Half looking for a follow-up email
from Juan, I check it first thing
in the morning.

There is one that quickens my breath
but it's from Wendy, not Juan.

"My parents told Brenda and Jackson
what they are up against
before we went to the conference.
      Not that they are going to die early
      but that they aren't going to ever get better.
It was a mixed bag. Brenda had a million
questions and seemed to understand
better than Jackson. She talks about it
more than he does. It opened up lots of questions
but also made us closer as a family
in some ways. It was like we could all talk
more freely and didn't have to worry
about keeping things a secret.
But sometimes I think Brenda
might be better off not knowing.
She dwells on it too much,
and I think it brings her down.
The things she says and questions she asks
rip me up sometimes.
It's a tough call and everyone is different.
I'll hope for the best
for you and your brothers."

The best?
All I can think of is
the beast.

NOT NOW, SAYS THE VOICE

I read and reread the email.

dwells on it too much...brings her down...
questions rip me up

      or possibly

closer as a family...didn't have to worry
about keeping things a secret...talk more freely

I think about the energy we—
      Mom, Dad, and I—
waste keeping the secret,
playing the "everything is peachy" game.

I know what I need to do.

The boys will be buzzing around at breakfast
but I need to talk to Dad,
get this off my chest.

He hides behind the paper this morning,
and I don't pay much attention
to the voice inside that says
"not now."

"Hey Dad, can we talk?"

He looks over the top of the paper
his voice not matching the cool stare.
"Sure, fire away."

I look directly at Davy and Trent,
tossing down breakfast but listening.
"I mean privately."

Mom stops puttering at the sink
as if she can feel the heat rising.

"I don't think we need to continue
the conversation, Claire." His words measured
and bristly as the paper he rattles.

"But I *do*."

"Will you two please take it into the den
and, uh, close the door?"
Mom's chirpy voice interrupts as she tilts her head
towards the boys.
Dad glares at her,
slams the paper down,
and heads for the den
without a word.

Proves my point, I think.
I follow him out of the room,
aware the whole episode
is blaring into the excellent ears
of my brothers.

HARD DECISION

Dad slumps into his favorite chair
more like the end of a long day
than early Saturday morning on a
holiday week.

"Why, Claire?
Give me your argument for telling
Davy and Trent how much
suffering they have to look
forward to. Tell me how
that would help."

I study his stern face,
hear the edge and the pain in his voice,
and wonder
what happened to the father who said just a month ago,
"We have lots of celebrating to do

when we get home."

"They're asking questions, Dad,
           lots of questions,
               I know you've heard them.
The seizures...the blindness...why Davy
is different from other kids
and who knows what will happen
when the whole nightmare
really begins to hit Trent.
Just the other day
he asked me
if I was going blind, too.
I didn't know what to say.
I'm tired of making up lies
and keeping it all secret
or trying to remember what I can
or cannot tell them.
It's not fair to them
or me, frankly.
It's just too hard."

Dad gets up and stands at the window
with his back to me for a long while
before turning back around.

"Hard."

          long pause

"How I wish to God
I could make it all easy
for you, Claire...
for all of us.
But I can't,
and for now
my decision stands.

Send them to me if they ask you
any more questions."

I know my cheeks are flushed,
and the tone of my voice is rude,
and my mother would call me on it
if she were here,
but I am finished caring.

"Sure, Dad. I sure will do that."

He watches me storm out without a word.

LIKE SALVE ON OPEN WOUNDS

I'm not sure which is more nerve-rattling,
my early morning convo with Dad
or the one coming up with Juan.
I try to put any expectations out of my mind,
but "third time's a charm" plays in my head
like the repetition of a broken record.

He settles into the booth
across from me
again.
I sense his warm presence
and connect with his smiling eyes.
It feels like salve on open wounds.

"So hey, let's try something different.
No music talk for now anyway.
Agreed?"

"Agreed!" The word escapes in
a gush of relief.

"So tell me about this conference.
It seems our recent conversations have
been uh,
in...ter...rup...ted
before you get to it.
Obviously it was awesome."

I gush some more
and get even gushier as I tell him about
all the hope and positive vibes
in the midst of so much sadness.

Too bad Dad has lost it
but I won't let that thought
bring me down right now.

"So, I want to be able to do
something. I know there isn't a cure,
won't be a cure for my brothers,
but if I could do *something*—
maybe raise some money to give
to one of the research foundations;
have some car washes;
sell some donuts;
you know, just *something*
to help, I would feel better.

"That's so cool, Claire, and
how are my buddies doing?"

"Sometimes I think they are doing better
than we are—
Mom and Dad and I—
but you don't need
to hear all that."

"I'm here if you want to unload."

"It's just that, well, Dad has huge
issues at work, you know, they're
putting pressure on him to expand the program
with less money, and that puts more burden
on my mom.
Things that were once minor adjustments
are now major traumas.
And the disease, Juan.
The disease marches on unpredictably
in both boys,
sometimes bringing irreversible changes
for the worse
right before our eyes."

Juan reaches for my hand
across the table.

"Count me in on the car washes
or whatever. Let me know how
I can help."

This is the Juan I've always known.

I swallow the lump in my throat.
"Thanks, Juan, for being there.
For listening,
for putting up with me."

There is a long pause
and then, "Sure, Claire.
I never stopped wanting
to be part of your life."

This time we leave the booth
at the same time.

I wonder
what law of the universe
allows you to end up on your feet
after your world turns upside down
and you've lost count of how
long you've been
in a dizzying tail-spin.

CHRISTMAS DAY

Christmas surprises me.
The grey shroud of sadness, exhaustion
uncertainty and dread
of the past months
            and the tension between Dad and me,
            and Dad and Mom,
lifts like fog in the face of sun.

Everyone, especially Dad, is
determined to be festive.
The day rolls along
full of laughter, holiday music
and an overload of good food.

Mom's smile is big
and she tries to hide the tears,
            joy tears,
that slip out during the day
as Davy and Trent take to
the gifts we so carefully chose for them.

The game, 'Bop It' is a winner
and for most of the day Nintendo sounds
are replaced by recorded commands:
            twist it,
            snap it,

turn it,
and shouts of glee as they vie
to one-up each other.
I remember other Christmases
when noise-making toys
tested everyone's nerves
by the end of the high-pitched day.
I can tell by the looks on their faces
Mom and Dad are soaking it in,
savoring it,
hanging on
to every sight and sound
for dear
life.

ENERGIZED

I wake up the day after Christmas
energized, thankful
that the holiday felt almost like
the "old normal"
and yes,
that Juan and I are

what...

maybe into our own
new normal?

I'm thankful for no guilt
when Mom and Dad
take the boys to Monkey Joe's
and don't seem bothered
that I want to stay home.

"I know you need to get some practice in,"
Mom says, and I flinch

when I realize how far down the list
of priorities
the recital
is.
But as soon as they leave
I put in some serious piano time
with "The Kite"
feeling reassured that I have it nailed
and then let my fingers drift
to Pete Seeger melodies
while pictures of car washes,
donut sales,
and Juan
float around in my head.

I think about how my friends
helped me through those first days
when we got Davy's news, then Trent's
      and now,
      Juan's sincere intent
      to help
      in a new direction.

I hop off the piano bench,
composing an email
as I head for the computer,
then I grab my phone.

Better check with him
before I invite everyone
to his house.

THIRD TIME, YES!

I try to temper my excitement
before composing the text.

Are we truly at this point again—
       easy access,
       breezy conversations

but no music yet, please—

or have I missed something,
jumped to conclusions,
assumed there is an open door
where there's still just a crack?

I go for it.

       What about a pizza planner
       with Mia and others
       your house Sat nite?

Immediate response:

       U r on, pending Mom's ok.
       BTW, you were right.
       Third time the charm!

Third time...

Yes!

EGOS AND POSSIBILITIES

Mia and I meet at the mall
for some serious Christmas exchanges.

"Big, Claire, this is big—
'never wanting
to stop being part of your life.'

If this keeps up I'll be forced to forgive
his ego trip."

"My ego, too, Mia. I'm afraid
we are two of a kind."

But that can't be all bad, can it?

"Hmmm, temperamental musicians
I'd say." She gives me a friendly jab.
Somehow her eyes and her body language
tell me I can stop the silly paranoia
about her and Juan.

"Yes, but there is something besides music
going on right now. Way better,
and safer to discuss."

We walk and window shop.
I try to compete for Mia's attention
to lay out my ideas about
making some meaningful contributions
and celebrating life.

She stops and faces me.
"I know you mentioned this before,
but you're really serious about it,
aren't you? And Juan is, too, it seems."

Now that I have her full attention
I pour on the excitement
about getting together Saturday night
to make some plans.

"I keep thinking of Mrs. Shepherd, Mia,
her comment early on, remember?
About mourning

instead of celebrating
the lives of her kids.
The celebration
for Davy and Trent
needs to begin

now,

and maybe,
well maybe
in some small way
we can make a little contribution
towards the possibility
of a cure

someday."

THE GANG'S ALL HERE

I realize as I ring the bell
that I haven't been to Juan's house
since the last time we practiced
          for Jazz Night
and like a kid playing doorbell pranks,
I'm tempted to turn around and flee.

So much has changed
between us, around us, within us—
but I try to focus on the recent turnaround
and force down the panic that
threatens to break out like a rash.

Juan's mom gathers me into a hug
before I step inside, and I can't help wondering
how much of the musical rift
between her son and me

has been aired in this house.

"It's wonderful to see you, Claire.
Don't be such a stranger."
She puts me at ease with her greeting,
genuine or not, and invites me to join
the noise downstairs.

I practically crash into Juan
standing near the bottom of the stairs.
          Was he waiting for me to come down?
The way his Cuban complexion
has absorbed his Colorado-ski tan
nearly takes my breath away,
but I'm really caught off guard
when he hugs me.
Mia, Kyle, Carlos and Tara
break out in applause,
          hoots and hollers,
as if this is being staged
but the genuine glimmer
in Juan's eyes tells me
it's for real.

My cheeks must be as hot
as I feel inside
and Tara, with her built-in romance radar,
hands me a soda.
"Okay, girlfriend," she says,
using her hands to fan me, "cool yourself down
and come tell us what this is all about."

TO CLAIRE AND THE CAUSE

I feel keyed,
almost pre-concert keyed.

The hug, the fact that my friends
care enough about Davy and Trent
to hear what I have to say,
the fact that what I have to say
is coming from somewhere
so deep inside of me—
        I fight back tears that
        threaten to let loose.

"Thanks for coming, guys.
It means the world to me."

I clear my throat
and pull out the feather and rock
and begin the story there,
gaining momentum by just holding them.
For the sake of Tara, Carlos, and Kyle,
I recap what BDSRA meant to me.
I mention the research foundations
that are already set up
and the possibilities of donating some money
and raising awareness through some school
fundraisers.

"Wow, Claire," Carlos says,
"maybe the researchers could find a cure
or at least some medicine
before... I mean, that would help
Davy and Trent."

I remember the presentations
on clinical trials at the conference,
and the reality of time that is required
for research.
"I can't count on that,
on seeing results in time,
you know,

in time to help my brothers."
That thought claws at my throat
and I feel like I'm going to lose it.
But I see Mia, fingers flying
across her laptop
like she does when something
grabs her
and Juan, his open,
kind gaze confirming our friendship,
and the other three smiling and nodding
their approval.

I can do this.

I take a deep breath and continue.
"Okay, Mia, unglue your fingers
from your laptop for a sec
and help me tell them
about our 'old' new friend."

Mia describes Mrs. Shepherd—
her colorful outfits, the way she talks,
her husband and children
and the family causes,
using all her narrative flair.

"So I have two things in mind that I hope to do
with your help," I say after Mia finishes.

"One,

to raise as much money and awareness
as we can to help fight this beast

and two,

to celebrate my brothers' lives

now, before it's too late.
Oh, and of course, to include dear Mrs. Shepherd
who gave us the idea."

I take a big slurp of soda and sit down.

"Here, here,"
Juan raises his can of soda
and leads a toast

"to Claire and the cause."

THE BEAUTIFUL CHILD FUND

Mia jumps in.
"Okay, y'all, let's start right there.
We need something a little sexier
than 'the cause.'
If we're going to grab some attention
and raise some awareness
about a rare childhood disease
we need a kicker.
The floor is now open."

Tara leads the way to the refreshments
and ideas start flying around the room
while everyone refuels.

Mia shrieks from across the room,
                mouth half full of pizza,
                nose in her laptop.
"Awesome! Claire, do you realize
what your last name means?"

"Well, duh, I suppose it's something like
a child who is fair."

"Better than that. Beautiful child."
    Voices escalate,
       brainstorming ratchets up.

After the frenzied calling-out finally subsides,
everyone flops down somewhere
and Mia reads the list off her computer.
The vote ends in a tie between
    "The Fairchild Fund"

        and

    "Fighting for the Fairchilds."

Mia gives an eloquent argument, pointing out
how the meaning of the name "Fairchild"
could be used in the publicity in all sorts of
kick-ass ways...

    The "Beautiful Child Fund" is born.

SOMETHING

Before the evening ends
we get as organized as a bunch
of loosey-goosey friends can get.

Everybody agrees Mia should
be the official records keeper.
    "Already on it," she says.

Nobody disputes Tara's expertise
in getting the word out.
    "Promotion's my thing," she says.

Juan agrees to check out
the school rules for fundraisers
       "and *deal* with the cash," he says,
        giving me a wary grin when he leans on *deal*.

Carlos and Kyle agree to fill in wherever.
        "We've got your back," they say
        flexing some muscle.

Mia and I will work on
the celebration.

The evening ends with hugs all around.
Juan's last, and most lasting,
seals the deal of our new
relationship,
hard to define but for the tingles
it sends down my spine.

Carlos and Tara carry the conversation in the car
better in the dark than on Tuesday mornings.
I totally tune out in the back seat,
thinking only about the

the possibilities

of

finally

doing

SOMETHING.

SAD NEWS

Sleep doesn't come easily after the meeting.
The warm vibes get crowded out by a taunting voice
I haven't heard in a while—

> *You don't have a clue, do you?*
> *No matter what you do,*
> > *it won't help the boys.*
> *There is no cure, you know.*
> *Aren't you really just doing the SOMETHINGS*
> > *to relieve your own guilt?*

I leap out of bed and decide not to fight it.
I grab my computer and the book I'm reading
and prop up in bed. I scan my new messages
and quickly click on one from Wendy.

I gasp in horror.

Hi Claire,

I'm sorry I haven't gotten back to you.
It's too hard to share such sad news.
Brenda is gone.
She didn't make it.
She got a bad infection
not related to the trial
and they couldn't pull her out of it.
Mom said we did our part,
we tried to help Brenda.
She said to tell you if your brothers get the chance,
trials are still a good thing
but damn, Claire,
it's so hard,
so, so hard.

Spend every minute you can
with your brothers.

I wish I knew how to help Jackson now.
He has stopped talking and eating,
wondering how soon his turn will come.

FORGING AHEAD

I wake up early on the Saturday
before Christmas vacation ends,

eyes puffy, throbbing headache.
The last thing I remember
is crying myself to sleep.

I creep downstairs for some juice
and find Mom on her second cup of coffee
looking almost as bad as I must look.

"What's wrong?"

"I was just about to ask the same of you, Claire.
Trent was up most of the night
and so was I, since your father's out of town.
I'm surprised you didn't hear.
I've got a call in to the doctor.
We've got to find some better meds
to help him sleep."

"I'm sorry, Mom.
You should have called me to help.
        Do I really mean this?
I, uh, had a hard time sleeping, too.
Thinking about school, I guess."

I give her a hug,
opt for a huge mug of coffee,

and head out of the kitchen fast,
before I launch into a tirade
about the boys' needs for the facts
and before I unleash my own grief
on her already-burdened spirit.

Wild, angry, determined energy
pulses through my caffeinated veins
as I vow to forge ahead
with the plans to do *something*.

The beast be damned.

HOW IT IS NOW

I scribble a to-do list:
    practice for recital
    Mia re: celebration ideas
    Juan re: plan of attack for school fundraising
    spend time playing with boys
    go for a run/relax

Satisfied with the agenda,
pumped by the caffeine,
I head for the shower
when I hear Mom's urgent shrieks.

"Claire I need your help, *now*.
Come quickly!"

I throw on a robe and race downstairs.
Mom is trying to get Davy on his side
    in the throes of a major seizure
while Trent sits on the floor across the room
crying hysterically.
Mom signals toward Trent

and I rush to him, gather him
in my arms, trying to make sense
out of his choppy, sobbing words.
Mom gets Davy on his bed,
the usual after-seizure procedure
and I take Trent to the kitchen
for hot chocolate,
what has become the go-to,
post-seizure routine.

"Davy wouldn't give me the controls
so I threw a pillow at him."

"Is that why you were crying so hard?"

"Yeah, because then he had the seizure
and it's all my fault, isn't it?"

I look at him for a long time,
biting my tongue, remembering my promise
not to tell the boys
what I think they should know.

"You didn't cause it, buddy. I promise you,
the seizures aren't caused by anything
either of you do.
Are you clear on that?"

He nods, smiles, and takes a deep, satisfied slurp.

"Um huh. Can we tell Davy that
when he wakes up so he won't be mad at me?"

"We sure will. Now how about
you and I go play
some 'Bop-it'?

When Davy wakes up
he joins us
as if nothing has happened.

The day is gone.
I've gotten nothing accomplished
      except for the most important stuff
      of all.

It's how it is now.

WALK IN THE PARK

Mia agrees to walk with the boys and me
to the park Sunday afternoon.
If we can slip in
some plans for the celebration
while the boys play,
I can knock off a few things
from yesterday's untouched
to-do list.

It's the first time Mia has been over
since the diagnoses.
She tries to hide her alarm
when Trent stutters a greeting
and stands too close to her
to make better use of his
dwindling eyesight.
Davy, on the other hand,
grabs his cane like an old pro
and says "let's go!"

Mia, always up for a challenge,
drives the conversation
with cryptic hilarity.

"What do you think about inviting
the flock to the shepherd's pad
for the "sheer" fun of it,
you know, for the big celebration.
We could celebrate her hundred years
and the two little lambs
all with one big
hooting nanny!"

"Ooh, great idea!
But we'll need to check with
the head shepherd, dontcha think?
Is she up to it?
That's a whole lot of excitement
for one old shepherd."

Davy and Trent roll the singing soccer ball
around near our park bench conversation.

Davy's perfect hearing picks it up.
"Are you guys talking about the shepherd
like in the Christmas pageant?"

"Yeah, sort of," Mia chimes in.
"What do you know about those
shepherds, Davy?"

"They watched over the flocks
at night. I don't know what they did
in the daytime, but I'll bet
they talked with the angels
that were bending down
close to the earth.
Angels are probly here right now
watching over us.
We just can't see them."

Mia blinks back something in her eyes
and hops up to give the ball
a swift kick towards the field.
She grabs each boy by the hand
and shouts.

"Come on, guys. Let's murder this ball!"

I follow behind,
loving my best friend
for loving my brothers.

MOMENT OF INDECISION

Mia shows Davy where to set down his cane
and we take over the middle of the field
in a noisy free-for-all.
She makes sure both boys get the ball
and I focus on potential hazards:
       rocks,
       holes,
       sticks,
       stray dogs.

Human hazards weren't on my list
until loud laughter off to the sideline
coming from two hefty guys in football jerseys
catches my attention.

One works hard to entertain the other
       with a sickening slap-stick
       using Davy's cane.
Now the other takes a turn,
marching around like a drum major
       or Gene Kelly and his umbrella.

My heart races as I try to chase them away
with a burning stare.
I know they see me watching them.
Are they baiting me?
I look closer.
Do I know them from somewhere?
I consider
       the situation,
       the size, the ugliness of these guys,
       the possibility of danger,
       and my brothers,
           obliviously
           enjoying this carefree moment.

Now Mia sees me and the scenario.
She keeps the game going with the boys
but mouths "Whadya gonna do?"

I'm frozen with fear,
indecision, uncertainty,
and then

horror

as I watch them use the cane
like a spear,
launching it into the highest tree
on the edge of the park
before taking off
like laughing hyenas.

Mia recovers enough to make light of it.
"Aw, would you look at that.
I'll bet a dog has carted your cane off, Davy.
I should have found a better place
to set it down.

I'm sorry about that."

"It's okay. Maybe an angel picked it up
and took it to someone who needs it
more than me."

Mia looks like she's about to have
another itching eye attack.
She tucks Davy's arm around hers
and guides him home
while I walk with Trent.
We listen as the boys carry on
about angels, shepherds, and soccer.

ANY MORE UGLINESS

When she gets home
Mia texts:

If something like that ever happens again
while I'm with you
let's take 'em on.
Jerks like that don't deserve
to breathe. smh

>Sure, Mia. The two of us
>against football biceps?
>And what would we have done
>with the boys while playing
>tackle football with two monsters?

Idk... Should have called cops?

>It crossed my mind.
>But I didn't want the boys
>to see any more ugliness

247

in this world
than they already have.

I hear you, but next time…

I stare at the words in my text
after Mia signs off.

*I didn't want the boys
to see any more ugliness
in this world…*

Is that what motivates my father's
decision to spare Davy and Trent
the truth?

any   more   ugliness

in   this   world

LATE NIGHT REALIZATION

Last thing before dropping into bed
I notice the to-do list from yesterday
on my desk, half buried.

Practice

at the top of the list
        didn't happen
                just one week before the recital,

    because

a walk in the park,

a singing soccer ball,
protection from danger,
shepherds and angels...

top priorities
in this present life

happened.

NIGHT WALK

Sleep is a long time coming
and I can't stop picturing the cane
flying through the air.

On this moonless night
my room is particularly dark

but not dark enough.

I get out of bed,
slide into my slippers and robe,
rummage in my bottom drawer
until I find the eye mask Dad brought home
from a red-eye flight to a European music conference
last year.

I put it on,
feel my way to my door
and quietly open it.
The house where I've lived all my life
suddenly feels foreign,
and I am afraid
that I will miss the top step
at the end of the hall.

I trace my hand along the wall
outside my parents' room
aware that my mother doesn't need
one more night of disrupted sleep,

but I can't turn back.

I feel a surge of relief when my outreached hand
finds the top of the stair railing
and I pause and grope with my foot
to find the top step
just like Trent did once.
Instinctively, I start counting the steps,
something I've never done before
and feel triumphant when I reach
number twelve and grope again
to confirm I'm on the hall floor.

Dad always complains that
we have too much furniture cluttering
the circular floor plan.
I shuffle toward the family room
picturing where the piano should be
and nearly call out when I slam into
an unexpected chair. Now I remember
Davy and Trent had moved some furniture
to play a game on the floor
and when I go around the chair,
I'm unsure where I am in the room.

Something crunches under my right foot.
I lean down, using both hands to sweep
back and forth on the rug until I find the small pieces
of whatever I stepped on.
I almost yank the eye mask off
out of frustration because now I'm afraid
I've broken something

I can't identify.

I try to pick up all the pieces,
slide them into the pocket of my robe,
and determine to keep going until I have
figured out how to get to the kitchen,
but now I am totally disoriented.
I bump into more furniture,
nearly knock a lamp over
and finally get down on my hands and knees
and crawl until I feel the cool tile
of the kitchen floor.

I'm tired,
frustrated,
angry,
already close to tears,
and totally unprepared for the thud
my forehead makes when it bumps into
the corner of the island.

I roll over on my side
moaning, trying to stifle the self-pity sobs
and the agonized scream
against the unimaginable darkness
that lies in wait
for my brothers.

TIRED

"Insolent ideologues who insist
on immediate ideas after
a Christmas interlude
are idiots."

We all look up from our lunches

at Kyle, the resident quiet guy
who has suddenly waxed so eloquent.

"You've been hanging out with Mia
too long," Juan says, laughing
just as Mia lands at the table.

"You guys talking about me again?"

"I think Kyle here is so excited about
the research paper we all just got
slammed with that he's turned
alliterative on us.
And we're blaming you, Mia."

Mia takes off with her usual
excitement over anything writing
while I stay out of the conversation.
The knot in my stomach tightens.

Preconcert nerves or something else?

Mia comes up for air and turns
toward me.
"You're sure quiet today, Claire.
You must be in Kyle's camp.
Hey, do you feel okay? You
look kind of puny
and besides that,
where'd you get that bump
on your forehead?"

"Yeah, I'm with Kyle and just
tired today. Never enough sleep
on vacation, you know what I mean?"
I pull my bangs down over the bump.

"Bumped into my closet door."

SICK

I slog through the week
like a flower slowly wilting...from what?

heat
        pesticide
drought
        neglect
root rot
        disease...

The cause is unknown
but the effect is real
and alarming, happening
concurrently
with almost daily seizures
of one brother or the other,
a mother struggling to stay afloat herself,
and a father being slammed against the wall
by an unreasonable administration.

Mia is ready to go with plans for the celebration
with Mrs. Shepherd ASAP. She tries
to get my attention more than once,
and I put her off with
headache or other ache
and "after the recital" excuses.

Juan, dear Juan,
gives me wide berth,
sending me texts to say
he's cleared most of the hurdles
with teachers or school officials

about our raising funds
and not to worry.

Everyone is making a big deal
out of the recital—the local paper,
radio and TV,
morning announcements at school,
huzzahs in the hall from Tara
and her cheerleading gang
and as much as they can muster,
cheering on from Mom and Dad.

The day of the recital my throat
feels like sandpaper and my glands
are swollen. I feel like crap.

Mom shrieks with horror as she
takes a good look at me at breakfast,
finally surfacing from a dizzying marathon
of doctor's appointments with the boys.

"Claire, dear God, you look awful. You're
sick. Why haven't you said something?"

She puts her hand to her mouth and
fights back tears. "Don't even answer
that," she says, feeling my forehead.
"I know it won't do any good to tell
you we should postpone the recital,
but tell me honestly, can you get
through it in this shape?"

Dad whizzes in on the tail end of the
conversation, his tone a reflection
of his own hellish week. "She has no choice,
Janet, this is too big a deal. There
will be college scouts there, the works.

You can do it, Claire, we know you can."

Mom's pathetic half-apology,
Dad's brusque dictum
leave me feeling nauseous.

The worst part of this morning
is the truth:

there is no comparison
between this challenge
and the one
my brothers
are facing.

I WILL DO THIS FOR THEM

By the time we get to the auditorium
I'm pretty sure fever is raging.
Monitoring temperature...pointless.
Water...small sips.
No bathroom on stage.

Thoughts spike like fever...

Davy's seizures?   What if I throw up, faint?
        Flub in front of scouts?
Damn.   This should be Juan's show.
                Get a grip!
Hold on.   Seven other students.   Regional winners.
    Only their composition.   Then me last.
State winner.   Three other pieces.
Then "The Kite."   Hold on.

Backstage resting head
against cool cinder block

soothing self
into what? Delirium?
Another wave
of panic.

Davy and Trent...
            I can do this for them.
Davy and Trent...
            I can do this for them.

But of course!

I *can* do this for them.
I *will* do this for them.
The rest of *their* lives.

THE RECITAL

Davy and Trent.
            Davy and Trent.
                        Davy and Trent.

My fingers bang the notes out.
I'm on remote control
from some far away galaxy.
I can feel the connection my
fingers are making with the keyboard
but the sound seems so far away.
Is the noise translating into music?
Is it making any sense?

"The Kite" swirls in my head.
Notes soar through the auditorium.
I ride them, feel the wind in my hair.

Davy and Trent.

Davy and Trent.
          Davy and Trent.

but then
like a sudden fork of lightening,

          a total disconnect.
Freeze.   Stumble.   Lost.
          A thick blanket of fog
long enough   to cause   a deafening
                    pause.

Finally
air rushes back into my lungs
forcing me to breathe, breathe, breathe.

My thoughts clear enough
to push my fingers
back on the mark.
          Keep going,
          we're almost there
and we,
          my fingers, my throbbing head
reach the final crescendo
to resounding applause,
          a standing ovation
                    that has never been
                              less well deserved.

I hang on to the piano, sliding
to the edge of the bench.
I shuffle a few feet to the microphone
where the emcee flashes a look of concern
without missing a beat,
makes the scholarship presentation,
explains the summer internship
to the audience,

and hands me the microphone
as if he expects it
or me
to drop.

I take a deep breath,
trying not to let my knees buckle.
I do the perfunctory thank-yous,
      especially to my little brothers
      in the front row.
More applause
and I faint
into the emcee's arms.

EMERGENCY ROOM VISIT

When I come to on the backstage floor,
      I hear:

"Clear some space, give her some air."

"...let you know, dear
soon as I can."

"Dad, is Claire going to die?"

"...call you from the ER."

"...going to walk her to the car."

I'm wide awake and alert by the time
Mom drives me,
way too fast and reckless,
to the emergency room
where it takes three hours
into the night—

blood tests, heart monitors,
head monitors,
stool samples,
questions and consultation,
with a swoon-worthy intern
to determine I simply have
a bad case of
dehydration
and strep throat.

"Heard you went out with a bang
at some kind of big music event
in your honor this evening,"
Swoon Hunk says, while he scribbles out
the prescriptions.

My blush gives the fever an energy boost.
I suddenly flash on the flub followed by the fainting
and I think I see where he's going.

Panic starts to creep up my spine.
"Okay, so, the head wires...."
"Do I have seizures now, too,
like my brothers?"

Swoon Hunk puts his pen down
and swivels on his stool to give me
his full attention.
In one of the most soothing voices
this side of the moon
he explains all the tests they gave me,
        the reasons why
                and the results.

"No sign of seizures," he says.
Mom's phone buzzes and she steps outside
to take the call.

"What's going on with your brothers?"

I glance toward the door and lower my voice.
"They have Batten disease, and, uh, no one
has talked to them the way you just
talked to me, and well,
I think somebody should,
but my parents don't agree with each other
and it's a sore point at our house."

"Whether or not your brothers are informed
about their situation is your parents call,
but your concerns here might be a good reason
for some dialogue. I'd be happy to
facilitate a family meeting.
Fair enough?"

Being in on anything the Swoon Hunk
facilitates makes me blush again.
I like this guy
apart from the fact he's gorgeous.
He doesn't
mess around
and he gets where
I'm coming from.

I nod.

"Just have one of your parent's call me
when the time seems right, okay?"

I nod again, amazed at how good
you can feel with strep and dehydration
at 3:00 in the morning.

FORGIVENESS

Mom tiptoes into my room
bearing six long-stemmed roses
and my medicine.

"Juan wanted you to have these last night
but he said to tell you
you need to practice your exits
a little bit more."

Her laugh masks tears
lurking behind sad eyes.

"I'm so sorry, Claire. I never
should have let you go on
with the recital,
as sick as you were."

I squeeze her hand.
"If you're talking about the flub
it's really okay. In fact
I think it's kind of—
I can't believe I hear myself saying this—

kind of funny."

"Hmmm, that's an interesting take on it."
Her look says 'maybe there really is something wrong
with her head'
along with relief and determination
to let it go for now.
She says she'll be back with
tea and toast,
our standard sick-and-home-from-school menu.

Dad pops in next,

and I brace myself
for his disappointment.

"My behavior is inexcusable, Claire,
especially in view of all the things
we learned at the conference. I
hope you'll forgive me for,
for pushing you when you were
obviously very ill."

"It's okay, Dad.
Really, I'm okay with it.
There's nothing to forgive."

Maybe if I don't tell him about
my new warped sense of humor
he won't tell me how unfunny
he thought it was.

Silence.

He smiles and leans down to kiss me.

HOME AND HOSPITALS

After sleeping most of the day
I'm pushing Mom to let me go back to school
tomorrow,
but she's sticking to her guns
about staying home one more day.

The hospital.
It's all Davy and Trent can talk about
when Mom lets them into my room
late in the afternoon,
            as long as they keep their distance.

Did they give you a shot?
Dad said they hooked you up with a bunch of wires.
How come you fainted on stage?
Do you have seizures now, too?

I try to give good answers
to all their questions,
remembering my promise to keep the secret
and thinking of the Swoon Hunk's advice.

I shudder to think how much
        hospital
they will experience on the road
they are traveling.

If only my brothers' health could be
restored
by a few pills
and a little bed rest.

Spring

THE REHASH

At lunch on my first day back
it's Kyle,
formerly quiet Kyle,
who seems to get bolder
and more comical by daily association
with Mia,
who is the first one
to break the silence
about the recital.

"Yo, Claire, your recital was...great.
Did you have to practice much
for that last part,
you know,
the grand finale?"

He practically chokes when Mia
kicks him under the table.
She looks at me apologetically
then *she* practically chokes
when *I* practically choke
laughing hysterically with my mouth full.

They're all staring at me
like I've really checked out,
          flipped,
                    gone over the edge.

Maybe more than one of them
remembers how crushed I was
when I took second place
in the regionals last year,
or how weepy I got after
I thought I'd messed up
on the all-state band auditions

even though I hadn't.
Maybe they all remember
how music has driven my life
since forever
and how it's rarely been
a laughing matter
but rather,
something I've been
dead serious about.
Maybe they expected tears
instead of laughter.

"You know I messed up, you liar,
so the recital was less than *great*
and yeah, I probably practiced more
for the finale than I did
for the whole show."

Well now I'm a liar, but I'm enjoying this
too much to stop.

Carlos glances at Juan
        who is staying silent,
then at me.
"You mean you, like, didn't plan that
um, long pause in the middle?
I mean, it's okay with me if you did,
I'm just sayin,' not being musical
and all."

"You got it, Carlos. I made a big, fat mess-up
in the middle of my award recital. Isn't
that a hoot?"

I laugh a genuine
deep down laugh
again.

"Claire, you're having too much fun with this.
Did you plan this out, or something,
for some warped reason...
a joke, or something? You can't be serious
I mean, about this being funny. It's, uh
not like you, you know what I mean?"

Juan looks as if Mia just took the words
right out of his mouth, and he stops eating
to wait for my answer.

"Okay, you guys.
Sure, it bummed me out
for a few seconds when I went blank
in the middle of my big moment
but you know what?
I flashed on Davy and Trent
and I can't explain it.
Somehow,
it seemed fitting.
It's like the new normal
in my life.
They count more than I do
or more than anything I can do
and maybe I needed
that reminder."

Tara jumps up from her seat
across from me and nearly stumbles
on the bench
to hug me.

"You've come a long way, baby."

I return the hug.
"I could say the same about you, Tara."

Juan aims a beaming smile my way,
leaving no doubt that the winter chill
is over.

The new normal.

MORE CHANGES

Mia catches up with me at the lockers
at the end of the day.

"You've changed, Claire."

It's hard to read her tone
at first, and then I see it
in her steady, straight-on gaze,
         a best-girlfriend version of Juan's
         warm vibes.

"Yeah, I guess I have."

I can't take it any farther,
any deeper than that
right now.
It is what it is.

As if she had been testing the waters,
Mia presses on with what
is really on her mind.

"It's about Mrs. Shepherd."
She watches for my reaction.
"She's okay, but, well,
I'm not really sure what's going on.
When I dropped in to see her
yesterday, to try to talk about,

you know, the celebration,
a nurse was there.
She said she'd had a stroke.
Not a really bad one,
but she...she can't talk
right now
or maybe

anymore."

"Time isn't on our side, Mia.
We need to do a Schmoozie's
ASAP
and get this show on the road."

"Agreed. Let's try for tomorrow
after school. You text Juan and Carlos
and I'll catch up with Tara and Kyle."

QUESTIONS WITHOUT ANSWERS

It's a constant battle
keeping up with the changes
rippling through our family,
our lives.

Just inside the door from
my upbeat conversation with Mia,
Mom tells me
      about her decision
      to take a leave of absence
      to deal with the boys' medical needs.

In the same breath,
      her concern that Dad is about to trash
      his tenure at the college.

One of the Tips for the Family
from BDSRA comes to mind:

don't let the disease always take center stage.

Is that what's happening?
Will staying home be the best thing for Mom
or our family?
How much of Dad's job problem
is related to the beast?

Questions without answers
and tuning in tomorrow
doesn't seem to bring
much relief.

JOY, PURE AND DEEP DOWN

Mia leads off at Schmoozies.

"Mrs. Shepherd has been moved to
a care facility, and she, we
may not have much more time
but I visited her there,
and she hasn't lost her spark,
just her speech.
And, this just came to me,
why not take advantage of that,
          not the stroke
          but the facility,
and see if we can have the celebration
there, in their big reception area?
It would hold tons more people
than her tiny house."

"Okay," Carlos says, scratching his head.
"But what kind of celebration
can we have at a nursing home?"

"A celebration of life, of course."

Mia jumps on it, "Why not a hootenanny?"

"Yes! Perfect!" I say.
The others give us curious stares.

After we take turns elaborating on
Mrs. Shepherd's backstory, zooming in on
the Pete Seeger events,
the giddiness spreads around the table.

"Oh, this is too exciting.
I could get the cheerleaders
to work up a special drill,"
Tara says, popping her gum,
"you know, like some of the moves
we learned at cheerleading
camp last year were all about
good sportsmanship, and being competitive
without being ugly.
I can see it now.
This will take it to a whole new level.
Can't you just see it?"
            She raises her hand to read
            an imaginary scrolling marquee.
"Students wage war on Batten Disease.
Awesome."

Carlos beams at her.
"Whoot! Whoot!"

Kyle starts humming

"If I Had a Hammer"...

Juan chimes in.
"Before we talk about the music,"
he says, clearly sending a huge smile my way,
"I've checked with the admins
and they are on board with helping us
do some fundraisers, all proceeds
going to BDSRA, of course.
Ol' Benson himself even said
we could set up some bake sales
        at the Spring track meets,
        the Spring Music program,
        the PTO meetings.
The sky's the limit, basically.

And Claire, about the music.
We've all been talking among ourselves,
and we think it's a no-brainer
that our first fundraiser features you
at the keyboard. A benefit concert."

I surprise myself with a quick comeback.

"Only on one condition, and that is
that we make it a duo."

He surprises me back.

"We can talk,
but I think that just might be
duo-able."

Groan. Chuckle.

Can this really be happening?
Have we reached that new place

in the galaxy where our separate
orbits don't collide, but fall into sync?

Juan hangs back while the others file out
and I'm suddenly aware
my hair is a mess and I have little make-up on.
I start to feel flushed when he gently pulls me up
out of the booth
and doesn't speak.
He takes both hands in his,
locks his gaze to mine and stares.
"I'm glad you're feeling better, Claire."
A flush spreads across his face;
maybe the first time I've seen him flustered.
He leans in and plants a gentle but firm kiss
squarely on my lips
and wraps me in a long, tight hug.

I'm speechless,
tingly,
saturated with joy,

pure and deep down.

EARLY CALL

I'm in bed by 9:00,
exhausted but pumped
by the day's events
when my phone lights up
with Juan. I blush
just thinking about the way
we parted this afternoon.

"Hey."

"Hey yourself."

"I was just thinking about you."

"Me, too. No! I mean, same here,
No, No! I meannnnnn, I can't stop,
I mean,
I've been thinking about you, too."

Pause.   Silence.   Breathe.

"Are you still there?"

"Yeah, but I forgot why I called.
I think it was to tell you
I *can't* stop thinking about you.
Yeah, that was really it,
it's that I *cannot* stop thinking
about you."

"Me, too. Well, I mean,
oh, you know what I mean,
          about you,
              I mean.
Right?"

"Yeah, I really do,
and I
love
it."

"Good night, Claire."

"Good night, Juan."

STREAMING LIFE

Calm, rested, recovered from strep.
That's how I feel lazing in bed
this Saturday morning
going over all the amazing events
of the previous day.

Spring is brewing outside my window.
A shaft of sunlight catching dust particles
looks like a conveyer belt
streaming life—
yes, life—
into my room.

I get up
and look in the mirror,
sure that I can see the kiss
smiling back at me

and

I study my hands,
hold them up to the mirror
and picture them playing benefit concerts
for my brothers.
For the first time
in a long time
I speak to these hands.

Not even Juan knows this yet
but he said he would help
and I know he will. I'll use
the scholarship money,
somehow,
as seed money for
a benefit concert tour

to raise more money,
lots of it,
for research
to fight beastly
Batten.

Just as the kiss rests on my lips
so does the music in my soul
rest
in my
heart
behind these hands.

TIME TO REFLECT

A quiet cup of tea with Mom
is long overdue.
It seems to give her a lift
      until I ask about the possibility
      of meeting with the Swoon Hunk
      to resolve the secrecy issue
      once and for all.

"You need to take that up with your father
yourself. I don't have the energy."

I vow not to react
and strike out in a different direction.
Without mentioning a word about
the plans for a celebration,
I just tell her more about my new friend,
Mrs. Shepherd.

She smiles.

The sun, the gorgeous Spring sun
floods our kitchen

encouraging each of us to open up
like new flowers.

I let her vent.
>Working part time might be better
>than a leave of absence.
>Dad might make it work at school,
>but things are still touchy.
>Davy's seizures and Trent's sleep issues
>seem to be responding to new meds,
>but it's one day at a time.

I sit at the counter long after she leaves
to get groceries, basking in the sunny room
and the time
just to reflect.

I think about how the icy finger
of death invaded our house,
our family,
my brothers,
just six months ago;

and how it threatened to steal
the oxygen from all of us
for a while;

and how it still lurks,
will always lurk,

but it isn't going to win
without a fight
to the end.

We will celebrate the life
OUT
of Batten Disease.

DREAMING NEW DREAMS

Davy and Trent are in a festive mood,
parading around the kitchen
and singing at the top of their lungs.

Mom and Dad just told them that their
dream wishes have come true.
Davy will be going to visit
the "Galloping Ghost" in Chicago,
the largest arcade in the US
where he can play video games
to his heart's content,

and Trent will be going to
a Dallas Cowboys game
to meet his idol, Tony Romo.

What they don't know
is that Mom and Dad will pick me up
at the end of the summer music camp
and we will all go together
to watch each wish
come true.

> *grieve and then dream new dreams.*

Was it grief or guilt that stirred
such reactions to my winning
the contest, going to the summer program,
accepting the scholarship?

Will I ever sort it out?
And now,
is it dreaming new dreams
that frees me up to
deal with it?

Who knows what can happen
when you set your mind
and your heart
and your hands
to work
dealing with
life.

DOUBLE DOSE

My mind wanders during classes.
       Maybe Spring fever.
       Definitely not music like it once was.
       Probably related to the Make-a-Wish news.

I wonder
how my parents framed it
when they told my brothers
their wishes have come true.

I wonder
if my brothers wonder
why they are so *lucky.*

I wonder if they'll ask me
if having seizures
makes dreams come true.

I decide to bring it up with Dad
       one more time
after an early supper
and soon wish
I hadn't.

Civil, controlled, but final,
he says,

"They are not ever to know.
Don't bring it up to me again."

I nod in reluctant agreement,
hold my tongue
and leave the room.

I entice Davy and Trent
away from the Nintendo games,
grab the soccer ball
and storm out the door
headed for the park.

I'm still fuming when we get there
and can scarcely believe it
when the two football jerks
already have the field.

They see us
and recognize us
and start laughing
and shouting obscenities as they toss the football.

I gather Davy and Trent close to me.
"Okay guys, looks like the field is taken.
Listen carefully. When I say 'run'
grab my hands and we are going to run
instead of playing ball this evening."

I wait until I'm sure I have
the jerky jocks' attention,
give them a double dose
of the finger
and shout 'run.'

I haven't felt so good in months!

GETTING THE SHOW ON THE ROAD

The six of us slide into our Schmoozies booth.
It's a perfect Springtime day,
the kind that usually lures you outside

but

on behalf of Davy and Trent,
my friends are here with me
in a stuffy restaurant,
eager to put the finishing touches
on a celebration of life.

Juan hands me the "duo-able" duet
he's worked up for the
benefit concert,
basically just the opening part
of the celebration.

"Piece of cake, right Claire?"

"Looks that way," I say with a smile after a quick glance.

I flash back on the grueling days of practice
before the contest,
before the awards recital,
our horrible misunderstandings,
both of my musical flubs.

Now everything about music
and about this moment
feels right,
balanced,
light as a feather and
steady as a rock.

Mia has visited the care facility,
worked out the details with the program director,
explained to Mrs. Shepherd that
she can expect a few visitors at her place
sometime in May
and oh yes,
she might want to take out those Pete Seeger records
and practice singing along.

"I'm working on a poem, a tribute to
Mrs. Shepherd, who gave us this idea,
and to her children,
and of course,
to Davy and Trent.
I'm jazzed, too."
She smiles big and nudges Juan.

Kyle has brushed up on his guitar
and is busy learning some Pete Seeger songs.
Tara has designed flyers
and is working the cheerleaders up to a frenzy.
Carlos says the wrestling club will donate refreshments
and maybe even put on a little demonstration.

"Whoot, whoot! I'll bet those old ladies
will love that," Kyle says.

After we all recover from a good laugh,
I try to thank them without breaking down.

"And there's just one more thing."
I look at Juan and then Mia.
"Will you two come with me, to help me
lay it all out to my parents? I think it is just
the right time for them to hear
some good news, and I want you both
to be part of that."

"Yes!" from Mia
with tears welling in her eyes.

Two thumbs up from Juan
and the smile.

FRIDAY EVENING

I ask Mom if Juan and Mia
can come over Friday evening
to work on a group project
for school.

She wears a new tired look
since going back to school part time,
an indication that things are still
too unsettled with Dad's job
for her to feel she can quit.

"Of course. They are both
part of the family, aren't they?"

My mom's a champ in my book
and Dad, well, we won't ever see eye-to-eye,
but I hope what we are going to tell them
will pierce the darkness
in their lives
like it has
in mine.

THE FIRST PARTY

I have that pre-concert feeling
like I did the night I went to Juan's house
for our "world premiere" party.

Only this is better,
because it's not all about me
or my music
and there is no sense
of competition,
but rather
the feeling that something big
and good
is about to happen.

Juan, Mia and I hang out in my room
until the boys go to bed,
and I breathe a sigh of relief when bedtime
goes off without a hitch—
seizures, tantrums, or otherwise.

When the house seems quiet
we do knuckles all around
and head downstairs.

Juan, without our having rehearsed
or discussed it,
takes the lead.

"Mr. and Mrs. Fairchild, do you mind
if we interrupt?"

Mom looks up from grading papers, startled.
Dad puts down his book, tentative, curious.

Juan tells my parents a lot more
about what I've been up to
than I would have
        but it's okay
because he's doing a much better job
        than I could
except for the fact that it's embarrassing.

I stay silent, trying to read their faces:
    stunned,
    amazed,
    excited,
and their thoughts:
    Really?
    Claire?
    Without saying a word?
    When?
    How?

Mia jumps in,
literally babbling
about Mrs. Shepherd
and the need to celebrate
her children,
their lives,
our lives,
Davy and Trent,
Now.

I tell them we are just waiting
to set the date for the celebration
sometime in May
but since it involves Davy and Trent
we wanted to check with them first.

Mom is crying softly now
and Dad clears his throat several times
trying to speak.

I remember the night the three of us
huddled in this room engulfed in tears.

When he finds his voice, Dad says, "Claire,
I owe you another huge apology. I was
reluctant to have you enter that contest

because I, well, I wanted to protect my little girl
from being hurt,
in case she didn't win.
I see now that someone with all this courage
didn't need my protection."

"No apologies, Dad. We're moving forward, right?"

He's about to answer when the doorbell rings.
Mia and Juan exchange glances.

Mom glances at her watch and gets up
with a worried look on her face again.
I think I hear guitar music before she opens
the door.

She barely has time to move aside
before Kyle leads the way in
followed by Tara and Carlos,
singing "This Land is Your Land"
at the top of their lungs.

Now I'm crying because
Juan and Mia
conveniently neglected
to tell me about this part
of the evening.

We all join in.
Out of the corner of my eye
I see Davy and Trent sitting at the top
of the stairs,
smiling and clapping.
Mom brings them down
and we finish the song.

"Are we having a party?"
Davy says.

"Yeah," Trent says, rubbing his eyes,
"How come you didn't invite us?"

All eyes fall on me.
"This is just a preview, guys,
the first of many
and you will be invited
to every single one of them.

I promise."

Afterword

I FIRST LEARNED ABOUT BATTEN DISEASE when Brandon, a student at the school where I taught, was diagnosed. The school served around a hundred students with learning disabilities, and while I never had him in my class, he was just across the hall, and I got to know him through playground, lunch and extracurricular activities. I remember him as a gentle, sweet third-grader with a constant smile on his face, struggling with an already modified academic curriculum, and then losing his vision. We teachers all watched in horror as he and his parents endured weeks of testing and waiting before the diagnosis was confirmed. He left the school and it wasn't long before we got the news that his younger brother had received the same diagnosis.

Flash forward five years, where my teaching career found me at a second school for learning disabled in the same community. There was a beautiful middle school student, Taylor, who caught my attention as her Teacher for the Visually Impaired escorted her through the halls. Again, I never taught Taylor, but all the teachers stopped to chat with her as we passed her or saw her in the lunch room. She was totally blind and her speech was fragmented and often hard to follow, but there was always a palpable sense of warmth and compassion extended to her by everyone in the school. Ironically, she was the same age as Brandon, diagnosed by the same doctor in the same month with the same devastating disease.

I felt compelled to write about the beast that wrings the life out of beautiful, bright children. I set about researching the facts and creating a fictional family in which the "well" teenage sibling deals with the new realities of her brothers' fate.

Batten disease occurs in an estimated two to four of every 100,000 live births in the United States, often striking more than one child in families that carry the defective genes. Early symptoms usually begin between the ages of five and ten and can include seizures or more subtle signs of slow learning, personality changes, clumsiness and stumbling. Eventually the children with Batten become blind and bedridden, and they often do not live past the late teens or early twenties. While medical researchers are getting close, there is still no known cure or treatment that can reverse the symptoms. Seizures can be treated with anticonvulsants and other problems can be treated appropriately as they arise.

The National Institute of Neurological Disorders and Stroke (NINDS) is the federal government's leader in brain and central nervous system research. In recent years, scientific teams are making strides in studies that involve gene therapy, enzyme replacement, stem cells, drug screening and more. Many foundations around the country are actively raising millions of dollars towards research to fight Batten along with 7,000 other rare diseases. Taylor's Tale, founded by the King family in Charlotte, North Carolina, is one of the world's leading voices in this fight against the rare disease. I hope when you put this book down you will go to taylorstale.org to see how you can help.

Acknowledgments

I WOULD LIKE TO THANK the two schools in Charlotte, NC that serve students with learning disabilities. The John Crosland School (formerly Dore Academy) and The Fletcher School each created a nurturing and supportive environment as long as possible for a student with Batten, the symptoms of which far exceeded both schools' parameters.

I am grateful for literary organizations such as Women's National Book Association (WNBA), Charlotte Writers Club (CWC), and Society of Children's Book Writers and Illustrators (SCBWI) that create opportunities for authors to grow in their craft and network with agents, editors, and other writers.

Thank you to my agent, Julia Kenny, who believes in my writing and worked with me to fine-tune this manuscript so it could find the best possible home.

Special thanks to my Light Messages Team: Betty Turnbull, Managing Director, who has patiently responded to all my detailed questions; and especially my editor, Elizabeth Turnbull, who has made the process painless with expert guidance, keen insight, and healthy doses of encouragement.

Thank you to Laura King Edwards, who willingly shared her family's experience with Batten and lent all the technical and emotional support a fellow author could ask for. Taylor's Tale, the foundation initiated by the King family, deserves huge credit for the funds it has raised to support invaluable research to fight rare diseases such as Batten.

Thanks to the Hawkins family whose involvement with BDSRA (Batten Disease Support and Research Association) and courageous journey have inspired many families who have one or more child with the disease.

Thank you once again to Carol Baldwin, the best writing buddy ever, for her early and professional critiquing and ongoing support across the miles and the blogosphere.

Thanks to young readers who offered specific helps when called upon: Penelope Chirolde for educating an old author on the ins and outs of texting; Gray Marie Cox, Julian Daventry and Olivia Rollins for their honest first impressions of the cover during its development.

Last but not least, thank you to my husband, Wendell, who carries my bookmarks in his coat pocket and graciously absorbs all the ups and downs of being married to a mercurial writer.

About the Author

LINDA VIGEN PHILLIPS finds passion in creating realistic fiction told in verse, to offer hope to teens and their families who face mental or physical health challenges. Her debut novel, *Crazy*, depicts the struggles of a teenage girl in the 1960s coming to terms with her mother's bipolar disorder. It earned numerous accolades, including *Foreword Reviews* IndieFab Book of the Year Finalist, the short-list for SCBWI Crystal Kite Award, and an Honor book for the Paterson Prize for Books. Linda's writing has been praised as "beautiful" and "emotionally impactful" (*School Library Journal*); her brave storylines "resonate with teens" (*Booklist*) and "speak to many, many readers" (*San Francisco Book Review*).

Linda enjoys conducting writing workshops, spending time with her grandkids, and advocating for better mental health through her involvement with National Alliance on Mental Illness (NAMI). She lives in Charlotte, NC, where she and her husband love to sit on the screened porch to watch the grass grow.

IF YOU LIKED

BEHIND THESE HANDS

YOU MIGHT ALSO ENJOY THESE TITLES

The Next to Last Mistake
Amalia Jahn

In the Midst of Innocence
Deborah Hining

A Theory of Expanded Love
Caitlin Hicks